Let It Go

DC Renee

Let It Go
DC Renee

ISBN-13: 978-1505580976
ISBN-10: 1505580978

DEDICATION

To my Babulya, who is **never** far from my mind or heart.
To my Deda, we miss you.

CONTENTS

ACKNOWLEDGMENTS

Thank you to my hubby, who supports me in all that I do and loves me like no other. Thank you to my co-writer, co-creator and partner in crime – my sister. You all wouldn't be able to read my stories without her. Thank you to my parents, who believe everything I do is magic. Thank you to all my in-laws who pimp me out like a boss.

Thank you to Jenny Sims – best editor ever (Editing4Indies), Rebecca Marie – cover creator extraordinaire (PDP Goodies by Rebecca), Carrie Sutton – wonderful teasers (Graphics by Carrie), Tiffany Marie – endorsement whiz (Everything Marie), and Atalia Melendez & Rose Tawil – promotions specialists (FMR Book Grind). I wouldn't be where I am without your help!

I have the best friends and fans (in person & on-line), who help me and promote me simply because they can. A special thank you to Marina Yermolenko (your feedback is invaluable), Sheri Hursch (if I have your approval, I'm relieved), Catherine Gray (there is no better fan), Suleika Santana (your support means so much), Janett Gomez (your encouragement means a lot), Rebecca Bennett(I genuinely appreciate all that you do), Jettie Woodruff (you helped start my writing).

A big thanks to Rachael Marquez-Landers, Nichole Hart, Elaine Hudson York, Jen Wildner, Jennifer Hagen, Lisa Pantano Kane, Tunee Harrington, Julia Katnelson, Margarita Auslander, Inessa Polushkin.

Thank you to a bunch of blogs (I know I'm going to miss some – sorry!) who rock: All About Books, Author Groupies, A Pair of Oakies, Amazeballs Book Addicts, Just One More Page, Two ordinary girls and their books, Sinful Thoughts Book Blog, Three Chicks and Their Books, Obsessed by Books, A Dirty Book Affair, Nichole's Sizzling Pages Book Blog, Red Cheeks Reads, Literary Love/Melt Your Heart Book Blog.

Most importantly, thank you so much to all the readers who took a chance on me and continue to do so!

OTHER WORKS BY DC RENEE

Stand Alone & Prequel to Let It Go: Let Me Go

A Brutal Betrayal

Coming Soon: Three Loving Words

CHAPTER ONE

Your brother. The words still echoed in Benny's mind after all these years. Not like he could forget his brother, but that wasn't what he was trying to forget. Most days he was happy...not exactly content with his life, but satisfied with where he was in relation to where he could have been. But it was days when he had to do something his not-quite hardened heart didn't approve of that had him thinking of the words he received that day. "Benny, man, I'm sorry...your brother." Today had been one of those shitty days.

Only a few of Benny's closest friends knew exactly what he had done. John, Chain, and Marco had been with him almost since the beginning. Marco was still in jail, but that was his own fault and for something that had nothing to do with Benny, so he didn't feel bad. The guy had been having an affair with the wife of a cop. Benny had told him numerous times that it wasn't a good idea, but the guy didn't listen. One thing led to another and the cop found out, pulled some dirty shit, and Marco was in jail for a whole slew of crimes that he didn't commit. However, John and Chain being behind bars was his fault. Well, not quite, but Benny had been busted with possession of a concealed and unregistered weapon. And seeing as that hadn't been his first time or even one of the first few times, he was going behind bars for a while. John and Chain were just loyal; a few punches to defend Benny, and the next thing you know, they had assault added to a few other crimes. His time in prison was all right, though. He had met Mason, the doctor who had saved him years before. He didn't really owe him anything when he figured out who he was and what was happening to him. After all, Mason was a doctor at the time and saving Benny was just doing his job, but something about Mason reminded him of Ethan. And that was enough to spurn Benny into action to protect him, to befriend him, and to be there for him.

Mason was now one of his best friends, but even he wasn't one hundred percent sure about what Benny did. He probably thought it had to do with drugs or something you'd find straight out of a mafia movie. No, it wasn't like that at all. Benny had started with a small time gang when he was sixteen. It was not as if he lived in a bad neighborhood, not truly, or that he had a bad relationship with his parents, or even that he needed the money.

His family was great, loving, cared for one another, but Benny just didn't feel settled. He was anxious all the time and didn't like his friends at school. In fact, he hated school. He was restless all the time and started looking for a way to feel connected to the world. At first, he became an adrenaline junkie, looking for new ways to get a momentary rush, but that always lasted only a few minutes. Then he turned to drugs, but that wasn't what he expected, either, because when he would come down from a high, he was right back where he started. He needed to feel on top of the world, so he got in with the wrong crowd, and the next thing you knew, he was a full-fledged gang member. He hated it and loved it at the same time. He hated what he did, hated the beatings he had to give, the dealing he started doing, the way everyone always had to watch their backs, but he loved the feeling of power that came with it.

Everything was fine for a few years or as much as it could have been. His family life had started falling apart. His parents did everything they could to get him out. They were disappointed in him, tried to make him change, and they even threatened him, but when that didn't work, they gave up on him. They figured that he was a lost cause, but they didn't want Ethan going down the same path. They had been right to feel that way.

"When you start acting like the boy we raised, you can come back," his dad had told him as his mom cried. It didn't matter because Benny had his own place by then. Benny sort of always knew that this was a phase, one of those "typical" teenage rebellion type things, and that when he grew out of it, he assumed that he'd be able to fix his relationship with his parents. He never got that chance.

The thing he also didn't realize was that once you're in, it's really hard to get out. He was working on it, trying to figure out how to make his way back to the "good" realm of life, but he never had a chance to do it. He never had a chance to make up with his parents, and he never watched his brother become something he wasn't.

He had been close to Ethan, always. They had their own issues and their own fights, but at the end of the day, Benny was Ethan's big brother and watched out for him. Except when he decided to join a gang. That had been one of the most selfish moments of Benny's life. He knew Ethan looked up to him and would want to be everything Benny was, but Benny had been too blinded by his need for power to even think about that. So, when Ethan came to Benny a couple of years later, asking to help him join, Benny should have done more. He should have figured out a way to walk away sooner, ran away even if he had to, but Benny had been in the thick of things then and had only told Ethan to stay away.

When Ethan kept insisting that he wanted to follow in Benny's footsteps, Benny finally had to sit down and talk with him.

"I don't want this life for you," Benny had told him.

2

"That's my decision," argued Ethan.

"Actually, no, it's not. If I say you're not in, you're not in. Got it?"

"Why is it okay for you to be a part of it?"

"Because I'm stupid," Benny admitted. "Because I'm not good like you. You're a great kid, E, and I don't want you getting involved in this mess."

"You can't stop me."

"E, you're not fucking listening to me," Benny had yelled. "I don't want you to be a part of this shit. It's not a good life; it's not the right life. You like school, you're getting good grades, and you're going to do something amazing with your life."

"I see the way the guys look up to you, the kind of power you have over them. I want that, Benny. Why do you have to control everything? Why can't you let me have some of that, too?"

"You see only what you want to see!" Benny roared. "It's not all fucking peaches and cream, E! I'm telling you, stay the fuck away from this shit! No brother of mine is going to be involved in this crap. Do you hear me? Do you fucking hear me?" Benny's voice had been so loud that he was pretty sure the entire neighborhood had heard him. But even after Ethan nodded, there was something in his eyes that made Benny think he was the only one who hadn't heard him after all.

He should have paid more attention to that; he should have relied on his instinct and made sure Ethan didn't get into trouble. But once again, Benny was too consumed by the rush that he was getting with the gang.

And then he got a call from John. "Benny, man, I'm sorry…your brother…" John's voice had trailed off, but the pain he heard in his friend's voice was enough to break Benny's heart. He had known, somehow. He had known that Ethan wasn't just in trouble or hurt; he was gone.

It took John, Chain, and Marco to subdue him after he terrorized his place, breaking everything in sight. His fists were bleeding, his eyes stung from the unshed tears, and his heart throbbed, willing itself to explode within his body.

Ethan had wanted to prove to Benny that he could be just like him, could make something of himself in that fashion. He thought that if Benny wasn't going to help him, he'd figure out a way to do it on his own. He went to another smaller gang and asked to join. They laughed in his face at first, but he was persistent, something Benny had loved about him until that point. They finally agreed when they found out that Benny was a member of a rival gang and was his brother. They wanted to use Ethan to get to Benny and then to the gang that he belonged to. They sent Ethan after some drug dealer in Benny's gang, but Ethan wasn't cut out for that kind of life. One thing led to another and they shot Ethan, in cold blood, like he was nothing. Like his life didn't mean anything.

It took two bottles of vodka shared among himself and his friends to get Benny to finally calm down. It didn't stop him from getting revenge on the assholes who not only shot his brother but the ones who set him up for failure in the first place. John, Chain, and Marco helped him dish out retribution for Ethan's death the very next day while their minds were still fuzzy from the alcohol they had consumed the night before.

That was the day that changed Benny. He no longer wanted to get out of the gang. He wanted to build his own and run the two who had killed his brother to the ground. He wanted the people not entirely involved to pay for his brother's death, even though, deep down, he knew it was his fault. He, and only he, was solely responsible for putting his brother in the ground. If he hadn't been thinking of only himself, Ethan would never have gotten into that situation. If he had stepped away sooner, Ethan wouldn't have wanted that kind of life. It felt almost ironic that in order to get the justice he craved to tamper his own guilt, he needed to burrow deeper into the life he had wanted to get out of.

He watched as his brother was lowered into the ground three days later, his parents an inconsolable mess. He had tried to come home and share in the sorrow and misery with his parents, but they wouldn't let him in. He figured it was their grief preventing them from taking comfort in their only remaining son, so he gave them the space they needed, even though it cut him deeply. When he walked up to his mother at Ethan's graveside, his assumptions were proven wrong.

"You're a murderer!" his mother screamed. "My baby is dead because of you!"

He was speechless, shocked into silence. She was right, but he didn't expect her to believe it, too. He was her son, after all.

"You don't deserve to grieve his death the way we do," she choked on her sobs. "We warned you, but you didn't care. You did this," she hissed. "You threw away our love, you threw away your family, and now you have no one left." Her words were said with a bitter edge that cut right through Benny. "Leave!" she screamed. "I don't know you anymore; you're not my son! My only son is dead, and you...you're nothing."

"I think it's best if you left," his dad added, pity marring his features. That broke Benny in a way that he couldn't describe. He had lost both his beloved brother and his parents in one day. And he had no one to blame but himself.

With nothing left to lose, his blood boiling for redemption and his life in shambles, Benny built his empire, so to speak, very quickly. His heart had found walls around itself where there used to be none, and he took no mercy when taking his opposition out. That was not to say that he hadn't had his fair share of punches. He had been in the hospital with knife wounds, gunshot wounds, and a number of other issues over the years. Ironically, the worst injury inflicted on him was a wrong place, wrong time situation. He had been leaving a club and managed to walk out right when some guy pulled a gun on a different guy he had been fighting with. Benny's arrival surprised the guy, who clearly hadn't ever used a gun before, and he shot him in the stomach instead of the would-be victim. That was when Mason had saved his life.

It wasn't until he became friends with Mason, the guy needing guidance and someone to be a friend and brother to him, that his walls started to come down and the man he once was started poking through. He had been trying to get his life straightened out ever since, but it was a difficult road to travel. Today was a perfect example. He wanted to buy a bar that needed fixing up and new management, but the owner was an older guy who had sworn the bar had been in his family for years. He needed to sell it because he had no one to pass it off to, but when he saw Benny and his many tattoos and hardened edge, he laughed at him.

"No way," the guy sneered at Benny. "My family didn't build this up so that it could become some place to sell drugs." The fact that Benny no longer sold drugs didn't matter, he wasn't going to change this guy's mind without some kind of coercion, and he couldn't do that anymore. He just couldn't. It did, however, serve to remind Benny of the kind of life he'd been living, the kind of life he got into, and the price of it. Ethan. That was the price of his life. And it had never been worth it. Too bad he had been too late in realizing it. The price of Ethan's life was never worth any of this, ever.

CHAPTER TWO

"Hey, Kitty Kat," Benny answered when he saw Kat calling, a smile instantly forming on his lips. He had hated her for a while after Mason had told him that she had accused him of rape and ruined his life. He had even helped Mason plan out his revenge scheme. It didn't take long for both Mason and Benny to develop a soft spot for her, even when they still both thought she was behind Mason's demise. She had wormed her way into his heart, behind the fragile walls, and he felt more human with her than he had in a long time. Her outlook on her situation, her cheery disposition, and her overall personality was a welcome distraction from the issues that he was going through while trying to clean up his act after prison. He had never viewed her as more than a friend. Not that he was blind; he knew just how beautiful she was, but he knew instantly that she was meant for Mason and him for her.

It had been almost four years since Kat and Mason had learned the truth, gotten their act together, and became a family. He loved them both like family and was incredibly touched when they named their little boy after him. When he saw the spitting image of Mason in his arms the first time, he vowed that he'd help protect this little boy the way he couldn't with Ethan.

"Hey, Benny," Kat's singsong voice floated through the phone and instantly turned Benny's crappy day into something much brighter.

"How are my niece and nephew doing?" he asked, truly considering them his family.

"Those two little monsters are doing great, crawling everywhere and getting into everything. I swear I lost five pounds just this week following them around as they explore everything they find." Kat laughed as if she remembered something.

"Bring them over and I'll give you a break." Those two had him wrapped around his finger. They called Katherine Katy so as not to confuse her with Kat and they called Benjamin Benji so they could tell between him and Benny. When Kat and Mason were trying to figure out nicknames, Benny had suggested BJ for Benny Junior, but they didn't find it as funny as he did. He did watch them often, though, seeing as they, along with John and Chain, were his only family, if not by blood, then through love.

"Thanks, Benny!" Kat exclaimed like he had given her the world, which was also why he loved offering to watch Katy and Benji.

"Did you call just to check in, Kitty Kat?"

"Well, that too," she responded shyly. "But Mason's birthday is in two weeks, and I want to throw him a little get-together. I need your help."

Benny hadn't celebrated his own birthday since his brother died, but that didn't mean he didn't love celebrating with his friends.

"Anything you need, you know I have your back," he told Kat.

They discussed the details and what he would need to do before they hung up. He scrubbed the palm of his hand across his face. Kat brightened up his day when he spoke to her, but he would be lying if he didn't admit that he was jealous that Mason had that every day. When he had a bad day at work, he'd come home to Kat, her smiling face willing away the painful thoughts and the vivid reminders. Benny had used his vengeance, his need for payback to push his nightmares away. But now that he was almost one hundred percent clean in business and the hardened edge was falling away bit by bit, the skeletons in his closet were haunting him more and more.

He took one more minute to dwell on the past before he forced himself to start working on his part of Mason's birthday. With the way his thoughts were working a mile a minute and the need to push them back, Mason was going to get one hell of a birthday party.

*****

Benny had been working on a new venture, a club that he was trying to buy. While working on the tasks that Kat had assigned him to prepare for Mason's birthday, the next two weeks flew by in a blur. He had recruited John and Chain to help Kat with her own agenda, not that they needed much convincing. They both had a soft spot for her, too; they just didn't acknowledge it the way Benny did.

Benny stood in front of his mirror wearing a black fitted suit and a deep blue button-down shirt. He didn't have many occasions to wear suits lately. He stared at the image of himself while musing that his rough edges didn't quite match the polished look. He could vaguely remember the way his eyes twinkled when he was just a kid, teaching Ethan to throw a ball, ride a bike, and even look up a girl's skirt. Benny chuckled to himself, remembering the shenanigans they got into. His mood was momentarily dampened by the realization that it was his fault there was no joy to be had with Ethan by his side. He shook his head to clear those thoughts. He needed to head out and make it to Mason's birthday. He took one last look at his attire. Most of his tattoos were covered. If you didn't pay close attention to the ones poking out from around his neck or the steel look in his eyes, he could pass for one of Mason's white collar friends. Funny enough, he used to be that guy. Squeaky clean, no tattoos, no drama, just a chip on his shoulder that he attributed to teenage rebellion. His body slowly started transforming into a picture book. Then Ethan got caught in the crossfire. And Benny got his first truly meaningful tattoo. All the others were just simply designs that he had liked or things he thought were "cool." This one was made to look like a puzzle piece was missing, shadowed in, three-dimensional, right over his heart. It had been so accurate, still was. When Ethan died, he took a piece of Benny with him. He took the best of Benny with him. Benny had barely felt the sting of the needle then, his rage consuming his thoughts, but it became an addiction, another way to release the tension coiled through his very body. Now, he was on the verge of being his own art showcase.

He sighed and headed out the door. The closer he got to Mason's place, the happier he was. That family could put a smile on the grim reaper himself. Even Eddie had started showing some of that charm, clearly letting Kat and Mason rub off on him. He was a good kid, but Benny was still hesitant around him since he knew he had been associated with Katherine, and he wasn't as generous with letting go of grudges as Mason and Kat were.

Benny had stopped by their place earlier to make sure everything was set up. He had gone all out, more than Kat had even expected. There was a cigar roller in the back, a tequila bar to the side, more food than you could imagine, decorations galore, servers, and a cleaning crew at the ready. He pulled up to the driveway and tossed his keys to the valet he hired. He had thrown a party for a hundred guests instead of the thirty they were expecting, much to Kat's chagrin.

"Mason deserves it, Kat," Benny had reasoned.

"Yeah, Benny, he does." She smiled wide before jumping into Benny's arms to give him a tight hug. As he held her close, she whispered in his ear, "Thank you for being there for him and me. We love you. You know that, right?"

He did, so he nodded. He loved them, too. He was never going to get to do this with Ethan or any family he could have created. It stung a bit. He had been thinking about Ethan a lot lately, and it bothered him. He looked down at Kat's smiling face and pushed Ethan out of his thoughts.

"Love you, too, Kitty Kat, but don't tell Mason I said that or he'll try to kick my ass."

"He'd never kick your ass." Kat smiled.

"I did say try," he chuckled. "I never said he'd succeed."

Benny had stayed to watch Benji and Katy while Kat got ready and then headed home himself to get ready. Mason's actual birthday was in two days. Adam often asked Mason for his help when Adam was swamped at his office, so it had been easy to hide all this from him with Adam's help.

Benny was fashionably late, completely missing the "surprise" part of the party, but he liked it that way. He didn't like the big fuss, and he knew

Mason would understand. He'd also have time to scan the crowd and examine the situation. It had become a force of habit to do so even in a place such as this.

He spotted Mason first, talking to Adam, John, Eddie, and some work-related friend. It was an odd group of people to mix, but somehow, Mason made it work. They had probably been talking about something medical anyway. You'd never know it, but John was smart as hell and loved learning. He had barely finished high school, but that had to do with the fact that he didn't like teachers telling him what to learn. He could read something and understand it immediately. That kind of knowledge was actually extremely helpful with the line of work Benny was slowly getting out of. John's massive size and his snarl might have helped a little, too.

He made his way over to them and gave the proper hellos, as well as wishing Mason an early birthday and apologizing for being late. He hadn't brought Mason's gift as it was being installed in his office the next day. He had ordered new computers, a new server, and some other technical stuff he was told was top-of-the-line and something any doctor needed. He slapped his back, talked a bit, and then made his way through the crowd, saying hello to those people he knew and side stepping those he didn't until he reached Kat.

"It doesn't look so over-the-top now, huh?" Benny teased as he hugged Kat.

"Oh, you!" She pointed her finger at him accusingly. "No goading me," she tried to say sternly, but the smile gave her away.

"Benny, this is Sophie," Kat announced, turning toward the woman she had been talking to when Benny interrupted. He had only gotten a glimpse of her, seeing as she was partially hidden behind Kat when he snuck up on them. His back had been rudely turned to her, he now realized, when he spoke to Kat.

"Sophie, this is Benny," Kat announced as Benny finally turned to look at a pair of deep brown eyes so dark they were almost black. *Exotic*, he mused. He only had a moment to analyze the face whose intense gaze he was on the receiving end of. Her full lips parted, as if in surprise, and her eyebrows knitted together. The look he was getting from those deep chocolate eyes was a myriad of emotions, none of which he could pinpoint. He would be lying if he weren't both perplexed and intrigued. But before he had a chance to hold out his hand and greet her properly, she pulled her own hand to the necklace at her throat and clutched it. Her lips thinned into a mixture between a sneer and a tight smile as she turned to Kat.

"Sorry, Kat, it just got a bit stuffy in here. I'm going to head out for some air." She turned on her heel and practically ran away before either of them had responded.

"What'd you do to her?" Kat joked as both their gazes lingered on the spot Sophie had vacated. She seemed so familiar, but he couldn't place her.

"I don't even know her," Benny replied.

"She's the new doctor in Mason's office," Kat informed him. "Don't tell me she was one of your famous one-nighters first," she laughed.

"Oh shit," he muttered.

"Oh God, Benny, say she isn't. I was only joking. That would be really awkward."

"Sorry, Kitty Kat. I have no clue, but there was something about her," he admitted. "Don't worry, though, I won't let things get weird."

"Good."

They chatted a bit more and then headed in different directions to continue mingling with the rest of the guests. Benny had all but forgotten about his odd encounter with Sophie, except when he'd noticed her avoiding him from across the room. Whatever her issue with him was, he needed to make it right, so he followed her when he finally noticed her heading outside. She was alone, and he took a minute to examine her. She had found a tree in the backyard to lean against, her head hanging down and her hands balled up into fists by her side. There was a faint glow from the lights surrounding her and Benny couldn't help but see how stunning she was. She pulled her arms across her chest, and suddenly, he wasn't at the party. He was at his brother's funeral.

He had been so distraught, so beside himself, especially after his parents had exiled him. He stormed out of there, but he remembered catching a glimpse of Sophie's sun-streaked hair as her head hung low. Her back was pressed against a tree for support, and her arms clutched protectively around herself as if in a tight embrace.

She had been sobbing. Backbreaking sobs, the kind that robbed your body of breath. He remembered feeling for her, feeling her pain, but he had been so consumed with his own that he looked straight ahead and walked away with John, Chain, and Marco following. That was the last time he saw her...until now.

Sophie. Sophie Basi. Her name echoed in his mind as the memories washed over him. She had changed, dramatically. No wonder he hadn't recognized her. She had been the girl next door, a year younger than Ethan, just a little kid. She had been tall and lanky, her figure just forming when Benny knew her, although her striking chocolate eyes had always been her best feature. He should have recognized her from that alone, but he had tried so hard to forget that life that it was no wonder he pushed her in the back, too. She had been Ethan's best friend when they were younger, hanging out until the uncomfortable phase when they were made fun of by their friends. She came around, nonetheless, but spent most of that time in the shadows with only Benny to talk to. Her keen eyes always had a knowing glint in them, like it was only a matter of time before Ethan noticed her the way that she noticed him. Her eyes had always drawn him in, and the way that she had seemed older than her years had intrigued him. While she wanted Ethan, Benny watched her. Ultimately, Sophie had been right because by the beginning of high school, things changed and Ethan no longer saw Sophie as a friend or the girl next door. He was in love with her, or as much as a kid his age could be in love. Even though by this time, Benny had been around less and less, he knew Sophie was Ethan's number one. When he realized just how important they were to each other, he pushed his childish fascination for Sophie into the recesses of his soul and the unreasonable pain of feeling like Ethan no longer needed him to the hollow spaces of his mind. After Ethan's death and his parents' rejection, he couldn't handle being around Sophie. It was his love for Ethan and his own feelings for her that had him asking John to check on her after he finally pulled himself out of his own sorrow. John had come back with news that Sophie wasn't doing well; her grief had caused her to get sick. It took all the strength he had not to visit her, to comfort her, just be there for her when Ethan couldn't.

He did what he could to help her behind the scenes. When John told him that she was finally fine, he had breathed a sigh of relief. It was another few months before she left town to start college. It had taken days of convincing from John and Chain to let that part of his life go. Sophie wasn't his problem. They were right. Thinking about her, worrying about her, had taken too much of a toll on him. It was like a switch clicked off inside him the day he agreed. He stopped thinking about her and that life. His memories, his feelings of Ethan, were harder to forget, but he managed just fine for a while. It was fairly recently that Ethan had been pushing himself into the forefront of Benny's mind. Like now.

He couldn't deal with the pain now as the memories assaulted him. He was on the verge of tears, and he hadn't cried since his brother died. He turned to leave. He wanted to go back inside before she realized that he was there; before he brought either of them any more pain. He must have made a noise or maybe she could finally feel his eyes on her because she looked up before he could escape. And this time, there was no confusing what emotions were written in her eyes. It was hatred. Pure hatred and it was directed at him.

CHAPTER THREE

Benny had practically run away from her stare and fled inside. He spent the rest of the evening avoiding her but seeing her had gotten to him. He did his best to hide his emotions, but every so often, he'd catch a worried gaze from his friends. He left the party earlier than he normally would have, but he needed to get away. He sank down on the sofa and just stared at the wall in front of him. His memories of Ethan crashed in his mind, and his body went numb from the emotion overload. He shouldn't have been surprised when he heard a loud knock on his door about an hour later and John's loud voice booming through. "Open up or I'm using my key." John, Chain, and Mason had keys to his place and he had copies to theirs. It had been as a precaution, so that if any of them needed to get away from their worlds, they could just crash at each others' places. But also because John, Chain, Benny, and Marco had locked themselves out way too many times when they were younger, especially if alcohol and drugs had been involved. Mason had been brought into the fold after prison, especially since Benny had visited and checked on Kat when Mason had been absent.

Benny made his way to the door and pulled it open, letting John walk in, although stroll was more like it. When they were growing up and were just kids, Benny had been envious of how John just poured into any space like he owned it. He had been a big guy, even then, and Benny had wanted to feel just as big. Looking back now, Benny realized that his need to feel like the most powerful guy in the room had started at a really young age.

"I was wondering how long it was going to take you to realize it was her." John spoke, his voice low and calm, but the hard edge that he'd had all his life was still there. John had gotten into trouble with Benny for two reasons. He was loyal and would have followed his best friend anywhere, but also because he needed an outlet for the life he had at home. He had learned early on to stand up for himself, or rather that you had two choices – take a beating or give a beating. John had chosen the latter, which was also probably why he seemed so much larger than his already huge frame. Not something Benny should have been envious of, but it's hard to tell that to a little kid.

"What the fuck?" Benny narrowed his eyes.

"Took me a little while to put two and two together myself. She's a fucking fox now," John smirked unapologetically. "But those eyes, man. That and the fact that she ran away from you as fast as she could when you walked up to Kat."

"You saw that?"

"I was watching her the minute I saw her." John chuckled and Benny couldn't help but smile. He would have watched her, too, if she hadn't been a painful reminder of what had been. "Damn, she hates you." John whistled through his teeth.

"Can't blame her. Seeing me probably reminded her of Ethan, and she couldn't handle that."

"Yeah, but that would have been pain, sadness even, but anger? You must have done something to her in another life." John paused. "I just came by to make sure you were okay. I would have come sooner, but I thought you probably wanted some time alone. That and Kat has some pretty hot friends, and I needed to get a few numbers before I left." He knew John would have dropped anything to be there for him if he needed but was thankful for his attempt at humor. Benny smiled.

"I'm good," Benny told him. "Some days it sneaks up on me. And Sophie was that today. Just going to grab a drink and head to bed."

"Good." John nodded and Benny looked up to see the pain etched across his features. John knew more about Benny's life than any of their other friends. He had known him since elementary school, whereas Chain and Marco didn't come along until high school and Mason much later. When something affected Benny's life, it affected John's, too. They had been as close as brothers could be without being blood. Sometimes even closer than Benny and Ethan had been, which ate at Benny on numerous occasions. But that also meant that when Benny lost Ethan, John lost him, too.

"Hey, you good, too?" Benny asked, finally realizing that this was probably almost as hard for John to remember as well.

"Yeah," John sighed. "Just sometimes...sometimes I wonder if his death was our punishment, but when I think about that, I wonder if it was for what we had done before his death or what we did after." He paused, but Benny didn't know what to say. He had often thought of that, too. "I loved him, Benny. You're my brother, and he was my brother. So don't, for one second, think you're alone when you're feeling the pain. You ever need to talk, I'm here." He spoke, looking Benny directly in the eyes before smirking and adding, "And I won't even tell the guys, so they don't think you're a pansy-ass." John knew how to make a bad situation a little better. It had been ingrained in him to do that, but right now, Benny appreciated it.

"Same here, Johnny," Benny chuckled. He only called him Johnny when he was trying to get a rise out of him.

"You're lucky I feel bad for you or you'd be on your ass for calling me that." John always said something like that whenever Benny called him Johnny, but he never did anything about it. "All right, I'm out." John started for the door. "Let me know if you need anything."

"Will do," Benny told him.

"And don't worry about Sophie. I mean, how often are you really going to see her?"

"Yeah, you're right. Maybe once a year at something like this. Besides, I don't mind the reminders of Ethan." John raised his eyebrows in mock shock. "All right, I hate the reminders, but I can deal with them if I know they're coming. Seeing her was just a shock. Next time, I'll be prepared."

"She's nice to look at, too."

"Yeah," Benny agreed before John headed out. He got himself a beer, then another, and finally a third before he headed to bed, hoping he'd had enough memories for one day and his dreams wouldn't be plagued by Ethan's lifeless body, or worse – chocolate brown eyes so full of hate.

CHAPTER FOUR

Sophie used to look up to Benny. The way he oozed confidence, how sure of himself he was, and how he and his friends all seemed to take up all the space in any room with their mere presence. He was awe-inspiring, even if he didn't realize the effect he had on people. Sophie might have even had some not-so-innocent thoughts about Benny when she was growing up, but he never settled. Even to Sophie's young and naïve notions, she could tell that much. It was a shame really that he didn't realize what he was to so many people who looked up to him, especially Ethan. Ethan was her best friend, then the guy who had "cooties", and then the love of her life. They had been young, but she knew that he was it for her. And Benny loved him like crazy, too. That was obvious to anyone around. So, she loved Benny. He had been the best big brother to Ethan…until he wasn't.

At some point, Benny had started needing more from life – more thrills, more rush, more excitement, more power…just more. That meant he was off finding those moments where he felt like he was the one in charge while Ethan was growing up and needed him more and more. Sophie watched as Ethan changed, trying to mold himself to be just like Benny, but Ethan didn't have the same confidence that Benny had. Ethan hadn't had that same carefree streak that Benny exuded. Ethan didn't even have the same presence that Benny had. That had been what had actually drawn Sophie to Ethan. He was quiet, but not shy, more like he was examining the situation, an observer in his own life. She had attributed that to being the second child and walking in his brother's shadow. He had been a happy child, the one who loved every minute of life and felt content just sitting and watching the clouds go by. He was never brash or harsh with his words, always honest, and never shied away from giving a hug or compliment just when Sophie needed one. He seemed to know exactly what everyone needed to be happy at any particular moment in time, except Benny. And it killed him that he couldn't just sit and watch the earth spin with his brother by his side. He never told Sophie in so many words, but it didn't take much to see that Ethan felt like he didn't quite have his brother's acceptance, even though Benny told him all the time how proud of him he was. But having someone say it and be there to show it were two different things. And then Ethan changed.

Benny started disappearing with his friends more often, then stopped coming home for extended periods of time. His parents hated it, hated what was happening, but they couldn't stop Benny. No one could, not even Ethan. They kicked him out after a while, but that didn't wake Benny up, and it didn't stop Ethan from trying to *be* Benny.

Sophie had spent plenty of time feeling Ethan's pain right along with him. Then she spent plenty more time feeling second best to the ghost Benny's vacated presence had left behind. She would be lying if she didn't admit that she had started feeling resentment toward Benny then.

She knew Ethan loved her, knew he adored her above *almost* all else, would die for her, pledge his life to her. He had told her so on numerous occasions. She clutched her necklace tightly in her hand as the memories of all the wonderful times they shared washed over her. Ethan had given it to her right before he died.

"I know I've been difficult lately," he had told her. Difficult wouldn't have been the word she would have used. They had been arguing frequently by that point. She had overheard part of a conversation between Ethan and Benny in which Benny had encouraged Ethan to join a gang. She couldn't remember the words anymore, but she remembered the feeling of pure shock, of rage, and a disappointment like no other. Her resentment of Benny grew tenfold with those words.

When she tried to talk to Ethan about it, he'd brush her off, not wanting to talk about Benny. And when Benny *would* call, Ethan would go running, and every time, Sophie sat home worried about whether that was the day Benny was initiating Ethan and what that meant for him, for her, and for them together.

"I know it's been hard to stick with me, but you always have," Ethan had told her right before he presented her with the necklace. "And I want you to know that I'll always be there for you, too. So I got you something to show you just what I mean." He pulled out a jewelry box from his pocket and opened it; inside was a simple pendant in the shape of an infinity symbol with a delicate chain on each side. "That's you and me. We're separate, but one. There is no end between us, no break, like a never-ending circle, but better. And it also represents our love. We're going to be together forever; I promise."

She had cried at that moment, the tears of joy overshadowing any bumps they had recently come across. They made love that night like they couldn't survive without being entangled as one. No other time, whether with Ethan or someone else, had compared to that night; the way their bodies melted into each other was something she had never experienced again. It had been burned into Sophie's very soul, for more reasons than one.

She never forgot about Ethan, their love, or everything they had done and created, but the pain lessened over time. She finished school, went to college, became a doctor, and even managed to date some people in the time since Ethan's death. There were rare days that something would remind her of him and it made her smile, thinking of him teasing her. But, more often than not, when his memory resurfaced, it forced her heart to break all over again. She had hated Benny since before Ethan's death. He had turned Ethan into someone that he wasn't; he encouraged him to join a gang, knowing full well that wasn't the life for Ethan, and then he got him killed. Sophie never knew the specific details surrounding Ethan's death, but she knew it was gang related, and that meant it was thanks to Benny. When Ethan died, she was too shocked, too destroyed, to even care about Benny. It was only after a few weeks when it really hit her that Ethan was gone and it was Benny's fault. The resentment turned to hatred, which bloomed and then grew and became the focal point of her ache. She was right to blame him, but it wouldn't bring Ethan back. It did, however, help her grieve. Blaming Benny gave her a purpose until she could move on with her life. Eventually, her life *did* go on. She got what she wanted, and she never saw Benny again. *Out of sight, out of mind,* she told herself.

Then he was in her sights and no longer out of her mind. She was poised and professional, and although she couldn't contain her false bravado completely when she saw Benny, she didn't let his presence affect her evening with friends. Not completely, at least.

She didn't drink much, mostly because she was a lightweight, always had been. Ethan used to tease her when they drank his parents' alcohol at the park nearby. She would never dare sneak her parents' alcohol. They were good parents in the sense that they gave her whatever she needed when she was growing up, but they were both stern and a bit aloof. It was almost like they had a child just to have one and weren't one hundred percent sure how to give said child anything other than essentials – certainly not love. Maybe that was why she had clung to Ethan so desperately.

After running into Benny, she was actually thankful that she was a lightweight, needing alcohol to numb her emotions, and numb them quickly; she had come home and drank several glasses of wine. It took two more days to finally push the pain and hate back into the little niche it had stayed in for the past several years. She should have known, though, that fate was going to be cruel and have her new boss' best friend be the man of her nightmares. *It's okay,* she told herself. *You just won't attend any more of those shindigs, or if you have to, you'll be prepared. And they will be far and few between, anyway.*

She snapped herself from her thoughts, wondering how long she had been standing in her fairly new office between patients when she heard a familiar voice.

"Hey Kerry, where's Mason?" Sophie cringed. *No, no, no,* she pleaded in her mind.

"Sorry, Benny, Kat called him and he went home because the kids were sick."

"What? What happened?" Sophie could hear the worry in Benny's voice.

"Katy was throwing up and Benji was, how do I say this…expelling from the other end." Sophie couldn't help but snort at Kerry's wording.

"So who's covering for Mason?" he asked, but by the hitch in his voice, Sophie was sure he realized what it all meant.

"We can squeeze you in with Dr. Basi, Benny. She's pretty full today, but you know we'd never send you away." Sophie could hear the happy lilt in Kerry's voice.

"Uh, thanks, Kerry," Benny spoke, but Sophie could hear the hesitation in his voice. *Good, be hesitant. No, be afraid.*

CHAPTER FIVE

Sophie had taken her time with the two patients before Benny. She had been putting off the inevitable, but she couldn't handle looking into the eyes of Ethan's murderer. Sure, Benny hadn't pulled the trigger, but he might as well have. She cringed when she finally opened the door to the room Benny was in. He was sitting on the exam table sans shirt. Sophie stopped in her tracks at the sight before her. His entire torso was covered in art, some leading up his neck, others winding around his arms. If she didn't hate him so much, she would have appreciated the beauty behind each image. There seemed to be no rhyme or rhythm to the images across his body, but they blended well all the same. Sophie had never cared about tattoos one way or the other before. She didn't mind them. She was never drawn to them, either, except in this moment, when a real live canvas full of art was on display for her. It was beautiful, each drawing made to seem as if they were alive, moving in sync with the owner. One seemed to stand out, one that had a blank space that surrounded it, no other tattoo touching it. A puzzle piece over Benny's heart. She knew deep down that it was for Ethan, and it pulled at Sophie, the missing piece, because she knew exactly what it felt like, for more reasons than one. There was a little voice in the back of her head that said Benny had no right to have a permanent memorial for Ethan, especially since he was responsible for his death. She instinctively wrapped an arm around herself while holding his file with the other.

Her eyes finally scanned his arm to see him holding his blood soaked shirt to a gash along his arm. That snapped her back to reality. She didn't know how long she had been examining his body; it seemed that minutes had passed, but had probably not been more than a few seconds. Around Benny, time always seemed to stand still.

Sophie went into clinical mode. "So, Mr. Negrete, tell me what the issue is," she started as she read his file.

"Come on, Sophie. Call me Benny."

Her eyes snapped to his. She wasn't sure what she was expecting to see there, something smug, that was for sure, but all she saw was pain and fear. It stopped the angry retort that had been on the tip of her tongue. She had no compassion, no remorse, for this man who had ripped her life from her, but the skills she learned as a doctor had been ingrained in her and she couldn't help the empathy that crept in.

"Benjamin Ian Negrete, don't think for a moment that you can be buddy-buddy with me. I know you, and I know what you did. So, while I am forced to treat you in Mason's absence, do not think, for one moment, that this means we are friends. If not for my sense of duty, I'd send you out of here." *Guess that empathy didn't last long where Benny was concerned.*

Benny started to get up after she finished her little tirade.

"What in the hell do you think you're doing?"

"I think it's best if I left. I'll put a bandage on it and call it a day." He smiled, but even Sophie could tell it was forced, tight, his words sounding more like defeat than arrogance. She hadn't been expecting that. The Benny she knew was always borderline haughty.

"Sit your ass down before I make you," she snapped.

At that, Benny seemed to genuinely smile before he sat back down.

"Yes, ma'am," he teased and chuckled. Sophie's eyes traveled to his abs, the muscles moving as his body rumbled from his light laugh. She hadn't noticed how fit he was when she had walked in. She hated the man, but she still had eyes and she could appreciate the state his body was in regardless of whom it belonged to.

"Why are you holding your shirt to your arm? Didn't they try to put something on it before I came in?" she finally asked, realizing how inappropriate that had been.

"Sure they did, but you say you know me, huh? Well then, you know I don't like all that fuss. I didn't even want to come, but the damn thing wouldn't stop bleeding, ruined three shirts by the time I caved and made it here."

Sophie snorted. There was the Benny she knew.

"What happened, knife fight with one of your thugs?" Sophie was only half joking as she sneered the words at him. He seemed to flinch at her question, his light smile disappearing.

"Something like that," he mumbled, a bite filling his words, laced with both pain and disappointment, even a hint of anger. She eyed him curiously. It didn't fit.

"So what really happened?"

"What does it matter?" he retorted. "I have a feeling you wouldn't believe me even if I told you."

"I need to be able to treat you properly." That hadn't been entirely true. Sophie had started examining him already and he had a pretty long gash, fairly deep, and would need stitches. But she wanted to know, call it curiosity.

"The kids next door were trying to build some kind of fort. Their dad was at work and they needed some help with some of the construction. They come to me for that kind of help when I'm home. They're good boys, but let's just say you shouldn't be around them when they're wielding any tools." He smiled.

Sophie felt the tug at the corners of her own mouth. She wasn't sure if she believed him, but that had been sweet. She briefly remembered Benny helping Ethan build things and "invent" things when they were growing up. She hated herself for remembering Benny that way, for even thinking about the good times that involved him. Benny wasn't that guy anymore; he was a monster, a killer.

She needed to change the subject. "You're going to need stitches. I'll numb you and then we can get started."

"No need, just go for it."

She just nodded, knowing he would probably argue until he won. She also secretly liked knowing that it would sting, and she would be delivering that slight ache. That brought a true smile to her lips, but it didn't last long. As soon as she started, Benny sat stoically, showing no emotion as if the needle piercing his skin was nothing more than a breeze caressing his arm. Sophie thought maybe that the amount of time a needle touched his skin to make the intricate designs adorning him attributed to his lack of response. She was also sure his lifestyle contributed to that as well. And part of her hoped that he was just a heartless bastard who didn't feel anything. No, part of her *knew* that he was a heartless bastard.

She worked in silence, but every time she glanced at Benny, he had a faraway look on his face, like he wasn't there with her. She wondered momentarily where he disappeared to, but she pushed those thoughts away. She didn't care, and once this was done, she wouldn't see him again for a long time.

"All done," she finally announced. "You'll have to come back to get those removed. Schedule something for a week from now with Mason." She stressed Mason's name.

Benny nodded, his face grim. "Thank you," he told her, his voice robotic.

She nodded in return and turned to leave, but just before she reached the door, he called after her. "I'm sorry, Sophie." His voice was no longer robotic but rather choked.

She didn't know exactly what he was apologizing for, but he couldn't possibly know everything he should have been sorry for. She couldn't face him, couldn't ask him what he meant. She ran out of there as fast as she could.

CHAPTER SIX

Benny had an aversion to Sophie, but it had more to do with the memories of Ethan she brought to the surface than anything to do with her. Truth be told, he had absolutely no aversion to Sophie in the physical sense. She had been stunning in a cocktail dress at Mason's place, but she had been just as beautiful when she walked through the door of the exam room in her lab coat. He could see just a small piece of black fabric at the bottom of her white coat, probably a skirt or dress, but somehow the two contrasting colors accentuated her shapely legs. She wore little make-up, either that or it had smudged off by the time she saw him and her hair was pulled into a ponytail. She had taken his breath away. *Where did the scrawny little girl go?* he wondered. She had been replaced by a woman, a very nicely shaped woman…with an angry scowl…directed at him. He figured that she wasn't happy with the memories he evoked of Ethan for her, either. He couldn't blame her, but the way she'd snapped at him, you'd think he had done something personally to offend her.

Benny hadn't been proud of what he did for a living, or rather, what he used to do for a living. In fact, he hated it and blamed it for its role in Ethan's death, but he needed it to get revenge and once revenge was complete, he needed it to survive, so it was a cycle he couldn't break. Until Kat came into Mason's life, and then, all he saw around him was goodness…goodness that he wanted to be a part of. Nevertheless, he never allowed his feelings about his life to show and made it seem like it was no big deal whenever anyone questioned it. But something about the way Sophie had sneered at him had his carefully constructed walls crumbling down. It took him a good minute to gather his wits and recover his façade. When he had explained to her how he had been cut, the look of surprise was both comforting and hurtful. Something at him tugged that it was nice to be looked at as a good guy, but the other part hated that this was indeed a surprise. Sophie had known him when he was growing up, and from what he could remember, he had been a decent guy and a great big brother, for a time at least. So why she was shocked that he could be that for someone else was beyond him.

When he felt the needle pierce his skin, he was sent into his hiding place, the crevices deep in his mind where pain equaled contentment. The sting of the needle didn't bother him anymore, not after so many tattoos, but he still remembered the idea of the pain, and that was enough to send him into himself. When he closed in on himself, he was transported to a series of flash memories, ones that involved the suffering he endured, the ache he caused for his family and loved ones, the heartache he deserved to suffer over and over. He was also treated to a series of scenes where Ethan was still alive and healthy, happy even, with a family and young children clambering into his lap and calling for "Daddy." The faces were always a blur in these snapshots, but this time, the face of his wife was Sophie. He could feel the tears building behind his eyes, but he held them back until Sophie told him that he was done. He watched her walk away from him and before he could truly think about the meaning, the weight of his words, he whispered, "I'm sorry."

She rushed out, unshed tears apparent in her eyes. She probably thought that he was apologizing for the memories he was causing to resurface, but it was more than that. He was sorry for the life she could have led with Ethan by her side, for the absolutely gorgeous kids they would have had, and for the white picket fence and house she deserved, but probably didn't have as a single, hardworking doctor. He was sorry for his role in all that, although she probably didn't realize it. He walked out solemnly after making a follow-up appointment with Mason.

*****

Benny had gotten Mason to remove his stitches at home. Mason had argued with him, but Benny didn't want to go back to his office on the off chance that he'd see Sophie again. Something about the way she ran away from him when he apologized had him wanting to protect her from any more pain that seeing him would undoubtedly cause. Poor girl had suffered enough. And she probably didn't even know it was all his fault. If she had, she would have spat in his face, much like his family metaphorically did. He deserved it, though.

It was another week before Benny convinced Kat and Mason that they needed a weekend away and he could watch the kids.

"Benny, you know I love you, and I trust you completely, but three days? That's too much," Kat had whined. She never whined. That was how Benny knew she was in desperate need of some childfree time.

"I'd take them for a week, and you know it. Besides, if they become a handful, you know I'll just call John and Chain to come by," he smirked. Those two guys were probably just as in love with Katy and Benji as he was. He always caught Kat's smug smile when John cooed at the kids, not caring what anyone thought. It was actually pretty funny watching a guy that was as big as a bodybuilder holding a couple of babies like they were precious cargo and talking in gibberish with a giant grin on his face.

"You're the best, Benny. I hope you know that. One day, I'll repay this favor when you have your own family and a couple of mini kickass Bennys running around."

"Kickass?" he mused, a smile on his face.

"Oh, definitely kickass. And don't forget that secret heart of gold only a select few get to see." She grinned.

"Only with you, Kitty Kat."

"Oh please, don't bullshit me, Benny. You do things on the sly not to tarnish that 'tough guy' exterior," she said with air quotes. "But I know you." She pointed her finger at his chest like an accusation. "You're a good guy. And good guys *do not* finish last. Exhibit A," she laughed as she pointed at Mason, struggling with the baby gear.

"Looks like he's finishing last now," Benny laughed as Mason cursed after dropping a bag full of diapers.

"Oh, stop it, you," she chuckled and slapped at his arm playfully.

"Ow," Benny howled.

"Oh shit! Sorry, Benny, I forgot. Does it still hurt?"

"Easy Kat, I'm joking," Benny snorted.

"I can slap your arm again," she threatened, a grin stretching across her lips.

"I could take you," he teased.

"But you wouldn't. You'd let me win and you know it."

"True." He nodded.

"Okay, fine, issue at hand," she started as she handed him a list of numbers and explained each one. "We're an hour away, so call us and we'll be here right away if you need us, but just in case, here's Sophie's cell. She lives about twenty minutes away. Don't bug her unless you absolutely have to, but if you have to, bug the hell out of her. If she gives you shit, tell her that I said I don't care. Those are my babies and if they need someone ASAP, they'll get someone ASAP," she added, steel in her voice replacing the previous lightheart tone.

"You got it." He nodded. Twenty minutes later, the kids were all settled in, and Mason and Kat were off.

*****

The first day and night, everything was fine. A little hectic, but fine overall. John and Chain had come over and they took turns entertaining the little munchkins as they cried for their mommy. Benny had watched them several times before, but never for so long, so he thought it was only natural to want Mom or Dad.

Half the next day was fine, too, but sometime after lunch, he realized Benji was silent, which would have been a good thing, considering the headache Benny was starting to get, but he was too quiet. He looked at him, and he looked tired. That could have been normal since he had slept in a new environment and had stayed up most of the night talking to Katy, but Katy was still talking to herself, clearly amused with her one-sided conversation about who-knows-what. He touched Benji's forehead, and the little guy was burning up.

He reached the phone and his first instinct was to call 911, then it was to call Kat and then Mason, which was funny, considering Mason was the doctor, but as his fingers twitched over the buttons, his thoughts became more logical. Mason and Kat deserved the time off. Benji would most likely have some cold or flu. There would be nothing either could do, even if they did rush home. He looked at the list of numbers Kat had left. He really didn't want to do it, but he knew he had to. He had to call her. Try as he might to find a reason not to, he knew it was the right thing to do.

"Hello, this is Sophie Basi," she answered after a few rings. He couldn't help but smile at how professionally she answered her phone, her personal phone.

"Sophie, hi, uh," he stumbled. *What was it about her that made him turn into a bumbling fool?*

"Benny?" she asked incredulously.

"Listen, I hate to bother you, but Benji-"

"Where are you?" she cut him off, her voice sounding urgent.

"I, uh, what?"

"Something's wrong with Benji. I got that much. You wouldn't call if that weren't the case. Kat and Mason are out of town, and you're watching them. Tell me where you are, and I'll be there soon."

She was so diplomatic and take-charge. Benny would be lying if that didn't stir something down south in him. He wondered briefly whether she'd take charge in the bedroom or if she'd let her guard down and let him lead. He shook those thoughts away, telling himself how inappropriate that was, especially with his worries about Benji.

He gave her his address and hung up, waiting patiently, or rather impatiently, for Sophie to show up. He wasn't sure if that was a good thing, but he had no choice now.

CHAPTER SEVEN

Sophie made the twenty-minute trip to Benny's place in fifteen minutes. She could have shaved off a few more minutes had she not gotten stuck behind a truck. She had been so focused on getting to Benny's place that she hadn't fully thought about the ramifications of seeing him again. He had rattled her with his apology, but she was able to push it to the back of her mind. Well, after a good crying session at home alone, she pushed it all back. Now, as he opened the door she had just pounded on, a sweet little boy in his arms and his brows creased with worry, Sophie had to hold back tears once again.

The scene was so agonizingly beautiful and painful at the same time. Sophie reluctantly remembered a time when Benny was sweet and caring, but that wasn't the same man who stood before her. And yet she had been trying harder and harder to separate the two Bennys she knew – the one who would have never sentenced Ethan to death and the one who did.

Benny looked at her, his liquid brown eyes so vulnerable. She had never seen him like that, ever. At the funeral, she had been too absorbed in her own grief and pain to really notice Benny, but she couldn't bring herself to believe that he hadn't been the cold, calculated, selfish monster at the time. That he had been vulnerable then, too, like she had been and as his family had been. Her heart ached for the fact that Benny hadn't been this scared for Ethan, for if he had been, he would have never encouraged Ethan to follow his same path. Her heart also broke for the child, the children she and Ethan would never have. That hardened her a bit instantly.

"Temperature?" she asked as she pushed her way in, not waiting for an invitation.

"One-oh-two last time I checked," he answered automatically.

"Katy?" she asked, her tone a bit harsher than she expected.

"She's fine. Finally got her to take a nap, but this little guy won't sleep. And he doesn't make a peep either." Benny looked down at Benji, the concern clearly written across his feature as he stroked him with his hand. Sophie's defenses fell slightly at the sight before her. Whoever Benny was, or rather, whomever Sophie knew him as, he wasn't that guy around these kids, around these people she had just recently started to get to know and really like.

"How about we check him out, huh?" she asked, her tone a little softer. She took him from Benny and when their hands brushed lightly, she felt the warmth of Benny's skin against hers and it sent a shiver through her body. She hated Benny, sure, but she was also a woman who hadn't had personal interaction with another human being in a while.

She examined Benji while Benny watched, hovering over her like a mother duck. She heard the telltale signs of his mouth opening and closing on several occasions, like he wanted to say or ask something but had stopped himself.

"His fever's down. One hundred, which isn't an abnormal temperature for babies. They tend to be a little warmer. He's got a bug, nothing too serious. You've been giving him children's Tylenol?" she asked. "Good," she responded when he nodded. "Keep doing that, watch him. Don't let him play too closely with Katy. We don't want her catching it. But overall, he's fine."

"Thanks, Sophie," Benny responded, the sincerity in his voice causing Sophie to flinch.

"Glad you called me. You never know what it could have been, and I'm sure a private plane couldn't have Kat here fast enough had you called Mason." She laughed and watched Benny grin widely, the anxious expression finally clearing from his face.

"Or the Secret Service," he added.

"She probably would have strolled into a police station and finagled an escort," Sophie chuckled.

"How long have you known Kat?" Benny asked.

"Not too long, but there are some people who you just figure out quickly," she answered his unspoken question as to how she knew Kat's personality so well.

"True," Benny added somewhat solemnly.

They had shared an awkward silent moment before Sophie said, "I should go," at the same time Benny said, "So, you want a tour and a cup of coffee?"

"I really should get going," Sophie responded, suddenly not as confident or as hateful as she had been.

"Yeah, it's just that you came all the way here. The least I could do is offer you something to drink before you go."

"It's all right, really." It was starting to almost feel like that moment when you didn't sneak out in time after a one-night stand and found yourself staring at the person whose name you forgot. *How do you let him down gently without sounding crude?* Except, this wasn't one of those situations at all. This was Benny, the guy who stole her life and dreams from right under her. The guy who didn't even bother sticking around to witness the consequences of his actions. He had killed Ethan and then disappeared. She didn't need to *let him down gently*. She needed to kick him in the nuts...hard...several times.

Before she could tell him off, she heard a wail coming from the other room.

"Hold that thought," Benny said as he strolled off to grab Katy while Benji lay comfortably in the playpen near Sophie, still quiet as a mouse. She watched Benny disappear into the other room. Strolling had been the perfect word to describe his walk; no, maybe swagger would be better. He walked with a purpose, a self-confidence that even most runway models didn't possess. She would have expected him to stalk, even clomp, around to emphasize his power – that even his steps were strong. She snorted to herself at that thought. That hadn't been Benny. He was always quietly sure of himself. He was the guy who you underestimated because he didn't look harmful but had a wit about him like no other. He looked the part now, though, at least his body did. All chiseled muscles and tattooed skin, several scars that marred his own personal canvas, and that glint in his eye that said, "I know something you don't know."

His body language and his tender touch with Katy and Benji, even his apartment, spoke of the sweet boy she and Ethan used to look up to. There were pictures of Mason's family scattered around the living room that she was standing in. There were a few pictures of Benny and his friends – some serious, some horsing around, but all fun. The room itself looked like it had a woman's touch – colorful throw pillows on the couch, interesting wall décor, even a plant in the corner. Sophie wasn't sure why, but that made her heart clench, a hint of jealousy seizing her. She reasoned it was because Benny shouldn't be enjoying life like this when Ethan wasn't, when *she* wasn't.

She didn't know how long she had been studying the room around her before she heard Benny's footsteps approach.

"Look who came to visit, Katy," he cooed at the little pink bundle in his arms. Sophie was a sucker for babies...clearly, and a sucker for big, strong men who worshiped said babies as if they were the only things left in the world, even if that man was Benny. Whatever hatred Sophie had started to build just moments ago dissipated instantly. "It's Auntie Sophie," he said as he handed her off to Sophie.

She took Katy and felt the distinct tug inside herself; it was the usual mix of joy and sadness.

"You play dirty." She smiled as she went to sit down, Katy still in her arms.

"Hey," Benny laughed as he put his hands up in surrender. "I didn't plan that. I mean, I'm good, but I'm not that good."

"Well, now that you're staying for a bit, what do you want to drink? Soda? Coffee? Wine? Beer?"

"Coffee would be good."

"Let me guess. Creamer and two sugars." He grinned and Sophie couldn't help but notice how handsome he was when he smiled. Then again, he had always been good looking –the older, sharper version of Ethan, but that was exactly why she liked Ethan more. He was gentler, softer, more endearing. Except right now, Benny was pretty darn endearing.

"Close, three sugars. And make sure there is a lot of creamer," she called out as he made his way into the kitchen.

A few minutes later, he came back with two cups and set one in front of Sophie.

"Thanks," she whispered.

He nodded in acknowledgment, and then came the uncomfortable silence. They sat staring at anything but each other for the next several minutes.

"Thanks for coming today." Benny finally broke the silence.

"You already said that," she tried to tease, but it sounded more terse than she had hoped.

"Right, well…I know that I'm not your favorite person, so I really do appreciate you stopping by. I just didn't want to ruin Mason and Kat's time away. They deserve it."

Sophie opened her mouth to rebut Benny's assessment on her feelings of him, but she closed it right back. He was right. He wasn't her favorite person, not by a long shot, but somehow, this moment didn't seem as horrible as she thought it would. Awkward, sure, but not horrendous. She chose to ignore that part of the statement. "I haven't known Mason all that long, but he works hard and his patients love him. So, I'd have to agree with you on not wanting to end their vacation early."

"You know," Benny smirked, "Kat pretty much said I could drag you here against your will if I needed a doc for Katy or Benji quickly."

"Like you'd need a reason to get someone to bend to your will." It was meant to be lighthearted, but as soon as the words were out of her mouth, she realized the deep meaning behind them. Benny had clearly understood, too, since he sighed deeply. "I'm sorry, I didn't…" Sophie started to backpedal, not sure why she would even be sorry for that.

"Yeah, you did," Benny responded. "It's all right, Sophie. I know what I've done and I know who I was. I'm trying real hard to get away from that guy, but sometimes, the past has a hard time setting us free. I could tell you that I'm sorry again, but somehow, I don't think that's quite fitting right now. And sometimes sorry just doesn't cut it. I don't think you'd even understand all I'm sorry for," he mumbled the last words, but Sophie caught them, barely. *No, he wouldn't understand it all*, she agreed with him. And he'd never know. No one would.

"Maybe I should go now," Sophie interjected.

"Yeah," Benny responded, his voice dejected. It made Sophie pause and second guess her decision to leave, but that only lasted a few seconds before she looked into Benny's eyes, their liquid color looking watery. She felt sorry for Benny at that moment, something she never thought she'd ever feel for him, which angered her. She steeled her spine, handed Katy back to Benny, and took a minute to check Benji one last time before heading out without so much as a goodbye. It should have felt good – walking away like that, leaving Benny to his own misery – but it only served to expand her own pain. That night, she drank half a bottle of wine before she finally went to bed.

CHAPTER EIGHT

Sophie had been jogging for as long as she could remember, but lately, it seemed like she had been pushing herself harder. She needed a way to divert some of that pent-up stress that Benny had been bringing about. She opted to run laps at the park a few miles from her home. Unlike most people, she liked to change up her running patterns, switch up the scenery, making it less routine and more about just getting away from life while doing something healthy.

She came to an abrupt halt after her first lap when she spotted Benny sitting on what looked like a blanket on the grass with Katy and Benji beside him. The sight of him – the bad boy so domesticated, a smile on his lips and a glint in his eyes that Sophie could see all the way from where she was standing stock still – had her heart beating a little faster. She almost had to remind herself that she hated him, hated all that he represented, and all that he had done. Her awestruck smile was slowly transforming into a scowl as she watched Benny play with the twins. It should have been her kids with Uncle Benny, but the better version of Benny, not this so-called reformed image that he had been trying to pass off. Sophie knew him better than any of his current friends, and she knew that he was no good for the people around him, especially the ones who looked up to him and loved him.

She wasn't sure how it happened, but she had found herself leaning against a tree, observing the way Benny leaned closer to Katy, making a silly face. Sophie snorted out loud and then quickly looked around to make sure that no one heard her. *God!* Benny brought out such differing and extreme emotions in her, literally within the span of minutes, and he probably didn't even realize it. She couldn't understand how she could feel empathy for him, amusement even, one moment and then an intense hatred like no other the next.

She hated the very thought of him after Ethan's death, after all she lost, and for years after, but she figured that she had grown up from such feelings. Until she laid eyes on Benny again at Mason and Kat's place. She berated herself because of those same emotions; if it were anyone else, she probably would have gone up to them to at least find out how Benji was doing, although clearly he was much better. Her instinct told her to go check on her semi-patient, but her regard for Benny stopped her. She sighed to herself, the petty side winning as she started to push off from the tree to continue her run. But when she looked back up, she couldn't hold back the chuckle that escaped her lips. Somehow, both Benji and Katy had started crawling away, which would have been okay had they gone in the same direction, but they were apparently trying to get to the opposite ends of the earth as quickly as possible, and surprisingly, those little ones were crawling very hastily. The look on Benny's exasperated face as his head whipped back and forth trying to figure out who to go after first, and maybe even how they got away in the first place, was enough to have Sophie covering her mouth on another chuckle.

Before she could stop herself, she ran toward them, scooping up Benji and calling out to Benny to go grab Katy, all while laughing.

She placed Benji down on the blanket and sat down herself, feeling a funny tingle when Benny's skin brushed hers as he sat down beside her.

"What are you doing here?" she asked Benny.

"I could ask you the same thing."

"Lucky for you, I was running around the park when I spotted you and your little dilemma." She stuck her hands out almost like a zombie, opened her mouth and widened her eyes and she swung her head back and forth, mimicking Benny's flustered look from a few minutes before.

She stopped when she heard Benny's thunderous laugh and she looked at him with his head thrown back, the muscles in his neck moving, the tattoos dancing along his skin. She smiled despite herself. She hadn't had a purely joyous moment in a while and this felt nice, even if it was with her enemy.

"I guess it was lucky for me." He smiled, the sincerity reaching his eyes, and it brought the corners of Sophie's mouth back up. "Benji had no fever today and had slept well after you left last night. It was nice outside, so I thought that some fresh air wouldn't hurt. This is the park Kat usually brings them to, so I figured it would be a good idea." He let out a dramatic sigh and clutched his chest with his hand in mock fashion. "I didn't realize how much more work it is. They nearly gave me a heart attack."

"I noticed." Sophie laughed. "I should have stayed back longer just to see what you would have done."

"Probably kept panicking," he teased with a smirk.

"It's not like they could out-crawl you. You just had to go for one and then go for the other."

"Yes, but if something were to happen to one while I grabbed the other, I'd never forgive myself," he responded seriously.

That stopped whatever clever retort Sophie was preparing to give him. This wasn't the coldhearted, selfish guy who was responsible for so much of her misery when she was younger. He cared about someone more than himself. It broke her heart and made it soar at the same time. Ethan would have been so proud of him, of the way he cared for these two babies as if they were his own blood, but it was too late. It didn't redeem the damage that he had already inflicted.

"So you live around here?" Benny broke her from her thoughts.

"A few miles away, but I drove here. I wouldn't be able to appreciate running around the park if I had been tired from running here already." She felt the need to explain even though he hadn't asked, and she wasn't sure why.

"You run here a lot?" It felt like small talk, but his questions were pulling her from her painful thoughts, so she indulged.

"Sometimes." She shrugged. "I run in different parts of the city so that it never gets boring. I hardly ever run the same route two days in a row, unless I'm in a rush."

"I like that." He nodded. "I usually just work out at the gym, get everything in one place, you know? I've never really thought about how the surroundings might affect my workout, but I can see why you change it up. It's a good idea."

"Uh, yeah, thanks." Sophie was caught a little off guard by both the compliment and the casualness with which they were speaking.

"Maybe I'll join you a few times and you can show me some good routes." She froze for a moment. Seeing him when she had to or by chance was one thing, but hanging out with the source of so much of her anguish was another thing. She registered the wistfulness in his tone, and it had her thinking that he was just throwing out an idea in passing, something to keep the conversation going. It made her feel a touch better.

"Yeah, sure," she responded, knowing it wasn't going to happen, but feeling better about not being the one to refuse. Although, why she would even feel bad saying no to Benny in the first place was beyond her.

"So, Benji is back to his old self," Benny stated.

"Looks like it." She looked at the little guy nestled near her legs, fascinated by the toy in his hands. "How'd he do last night?"

"I gave him some more Tylenol, and he was out like a light after that. Slept almost the entire night. Woke up like a changed man this morning." Benny smiled.

"Changed man, huh?" she giggled.

"Oh, definitely. What do you think he was doing when you scooped him up? He saw a pretty girl and went after her. He's learning from his uncle."

It hurt a bit to hear him say "uncle," but his sly smile and the fact that they were making small talk seem painless had her going along with him. "Oh, is that right? And if he was going after pretty girls, what was Katy doing?"

"The girl's smart. She was crawling away from me as far and fast as she could go."

Benny kept a smile on his face, but his tone had changed from lighthearted to something a little heavier. She didn't want to think about it or the truth behind his words. She was enjoying time with the guy she once knew rather than the monster he had become. So, she chose to ignore the meaning of his sentence and continue their playful attitude. "Then I guess she must have been learning from me." She smiled wide.

Benny's smile seemed to falter for a moment and Sophie wondered whether the truth in her statement might override the joking nature of it. Benny's lips tipped back up and Sophie breathed a sigh of relief. "Like I said, a smart girl," he chuckled. "I'm sure Mason would be happy to know his baby girl is already running away from men. You might have to take her under your wing and teach her a thing or two about how to spot a good guy. I'd say that's Kat's job, but hell, she picked Mason, so Katy's bound to be hopeless."

She hadn't needed to be around Benny more than a couple of times to know he absolutely adored Kat and Mason and thought the world of them. "Watch it, Mister, that's my boss you're talking about."

"I'll put in a good word for you," he laughed.

Sophie opened her mouth to retort, but just then Katy let out a loud wail. "I guess that's your cue to go home. I'd better get a move on, too. Someone interrupted my run," she stressed in mock sarcasm.

"Can't blame me. It was all them." He laughed and pointed to the two squirming babies he was trying to wrestle with.

"All right, well, good luck," she said as she started to walk off, feeling a bit awkward all of a sudden.

"Hey, Sophie," he called out.

"Yeah?"

He opened his mouth and then shut it and then opened it again before finally saying, "It was great seeing you again." He paused. "I mean, like this."

"Yeah, Benny, it was," she agreed and walked off back toward the path to continue her run and get her mind into a numb place.

CHAPTER NINE

Benny spent the next couple weeks busy trying to buy out a club. This time around, the current owner was more receptive to Benny and things had been going relatively smoothly. He hadn't had time to think about Sophie or the way she made him feel. Every time he was around her, a mixture of pain and relief surrounded him. He felt like she truly understood his suffering from the loss of Ethan, and he liked the bright memories her presence brought about. He also hated that he thought about Ethan a lot more when she was around. Her mood swings around him also were confusing as hell. One minute, she would be bright and shined like a king's treasure, her beauty stunning him into acting like an awkward teenager – and he had never been an awkward teenager. When her bright brown eyes shined on him, he couldn't help the desire that coursed through his veins. But when her tongue lashed out at him, it actually intrigued him more. She was feisty and he liked that. She kind of reminded him of Kat. Although Kat was like a sister to him, he appreciated her and told himself the day he met her that if he was ever going to settle down, it would be with a girl like her, and Sophie seemed to be hitting the nail on that one.

Mason had called Benny earlier that day to see if he wanted to come over and hang out since Kat was going out. What Mason was really asking was whether Benny would help him watch the twins. Like Benny could ever say no to Mason or his niece and nephew.

John and Chain had come over, too, and between the four of them, the twins were in good hands. After they had gone to bed, the guys hung out like old times, watching TV and laughing while drinking beers.

"So you let her off the leash," John had joked about Kat going out. Both John and Chain were pretty quiet guys, but get them riled up or drinking, and you'd think they were out to make new friends. They were fun and free, and John thought he was funny. He wasn't really, but Benny loved the guy anyway.

"Nah, Kat's clever, she probably figured out how to open the collar herself," Chain laughed.

"Or wiggled out," John chuckled.

Yep, neither were really funny.

"Hey! That's my wife you guys are talking about."

"We're saying she's smart," Chain retorted, a smile on his face.

"Whatever," mumbled Mason.

"Where's Kat anyway?" Chain asked. Mason had told Benny that she'd gone out with a girlfriend but hadn't said much else. Considering the life that Kat had led before she met Mason, not to mention the time she spent pretty much imprisoned in Mason's home, Benny was always glad to hear about Kat going out with friends. She was such an amazing person and it was a wonder she hadn't had many friends before they all met her. She needed people to lean on, and she was slowly blossoming. It was a pleasure to watch it all happen.

"You remember the new doc, Sophie, working for me?"

"Yep," John said, tight-lipped. Sophie's new presence to the group had affected him as well. She was just as much a reminder of Ethan to him as she was to Benny. Chain had nodded. He knew who she was as well, but it hadn't had the same effect on him.

"Well, you know Kat when she gets an idea, and she's had her eye on making Sophie her new friend since she met her. She badgered her to go out until Sophie finally relented. They're off getting drunk somewhere."

Benny chuckled to himself. Kat was hard to say no to. He was pretty impressed that Sophie hadn't caved sooner. It made him appreciate her just a tiny bit more.

They spent another few hours horsing around before John and Chain called it a night. Benny stayed a little longer to help Mason clean up. He was just about to head out when Mason's phone rang.

"Hey, Kat," Mason spoke. Benny couldn't hear what Kat was saying on the other end, but it sounded loud and a little slurred.

He listened as Mason tried to understand what she was saying while laughing at whatever it was that he heard. Finally, he hung up and turned to Benny, a grimace on his face.

Benny had heard enough to figure out that Kat was drunk and needed a ride home. He was pretty sure Kat offered to take a cab home, but Mason wasn't having it.

"I got it," Benny said.

"You sure? I'd go, but I can't leave the kids. Unless you want to stay and I'll go?"

"Nah, don't worry about it. Be back soon." He got the address and strode out the door.

Benny prided himself on being a smart guy, but he hadn't realized that a drunk Kat probably meant a drunk Sophie. He wasn't prepared when he came face to face with a smoking hot, fairly inebriated Sophie. Kat was just as gorgeous as ever, but she didn't get his blood plumping.

"Hey, Kitty Kat," he said as he found the two girls sitting on a bench outside of some bar. "Sophie," he nodded.

"Benny!" Kat screeched. "I love you, Benny! You're a great guy for coming to get us, even though you've been a meanie before."

Benny had seen Kat hammered only a handful of times and each time was a riot. She was a very happy drunk. She, unlike John and Chain, was funny, and she didn't really try.

"All right, Kat, in you go." He ushered her into the car before going back for Sophie. She seemed melancholy, not a bubbly drunk at all. Her downcast eyes allowed him to scan her for a minute. She was wearing a short black dress that hugged her curves like a second skin. It was long sleeve and high cut, which somehow made it more alluring. Her dark brown hair was flowing freely around her shoulders. When he went to help her up, she looked up at him through her lashes and he nearly died. They were watery and despair was written across them, but they were bright with the emotions she was feeling. Her smoky green eyeshadow only emphasized the green flakes within her deep brown eyes. He put his hand on her back and it was then that he realized the true intrigue of the dress. It was backless and her skin was hot to the touch even though the night had turned a bit chilly. He felt the smooth curve of her spine as he helped her into the car, his eyes shamelessly roaming over her body.

"Kat, I know where you live, but Sophie, you'll have to tell me your address," he told the girls as he got in.

"Sophie doesn't like you very much," Kat tried to whisper and failed miserably as she leaned closer to Benny. "Shhh, don't tell her that I told you."

"I think you're right," Benny said, trying to hide his smile from Kat's antics as he looked at Sophie in his rearview mirror. She was staring straight at him, her eyes full of fire now.

"We should go dancing!" Kat announced.

"No more dancing for tonight," Benny responded.

"I'll dance with Mase! He'll dance with me, right Benny?"

"He'll do anything you want, Kitty Kat. You have him wrapped around your finger. I'd tell you not to tell him that, but I'm sure he knows it. You also probably won't remember this tomorrow anyway."

"Okay, Benny." She smiled. "I really do love you." Apparently, Kat was also a very loving drunk, too. "But you have ghosts in your closet."

"You mean skeletons?" he asked.

"Yeah!" She snapped her fingers like she had just thought of something special. "Yeah, skeletons. You should get rid of them."

He wasn't sure what in the heck Kat was talking about, but he attributed it to the alcohol talking. Besides, she knew enough about his shady past to know he had plenty of skeletons collecting dust. He wondered why she was bringing it up now, but he didn't think he'd get anywhere having a serious conversation with her.

"I'm trying," he responded seriously. He really was trying to break away from his life. He was pretty much there.

"Here we go," Benny said as they made their way to Kat's place. Mason must have been watching for them because he bounded out the door as soon as they pulled up.

"Mase! Can we pretend it's your birthday?" Kat giggled.

"Maybe tomorrow." He wrinkled his nose and tried unsuccessfully to stifle a laugh.

All Benny knew was that when Kat was still being held captive by Mason, she had surprised him with a birthday he'd never forget, and ever since, Mason loved his birthday. It didn't take much for Benny to figure out that whatever it was hadn't involved clothes.

He watched them make their way inside after Mason thanked him. He turned to Sophie and asked her for her address. She reluctantly gave it to him, and he looked it up.

"Did you have fun tonight?" he asked, trying to make the drive a little less awkward.

"Yep," she popped the "p."

"Kat's great. Glad you guys are friends."

"I like her," she stated, no emotion present in her voice.

"She takes care of her own, and it looks like she's taken you under her wing, so you're golden." Benny meant every word he said, even if Sophie didn't care.

The drive to Sophie's wasn't that long. She lived close to Mason and Kat, but it felt like it took hours.

"Thanks for picking us up," Sophie spoke as they reached her place.

"Any time."

She started to get out of the car but wobbled on her legs. "Here, let me help," Benny started after her, but she pushed him away.

"I don't need your help."

"I know, but I'm giving it to you anyway."

"I don't want it." She slapped his hands away.

"You just thanked me for picking you and Kat up." He pointed out the hypocrisy behind her words as he followed her to her door, holding his hands just a breath away from her body in case she stumbled.

"That was different. That was for Kat," she sneered as she struggled to open her door.

"Yeah, well, it looks like you need me again." He pointed at the key, his words carrying more meaning than she would know.

"I don't want your help!" she screamed. She probably hadn't wanted it years before, either, but that hadn't stopped him, whether she knew it or not.

"Shhh, keep it down," he spoke as he grabbed the key from her hand and opened the door. "Fine, you don't need my help, you don't want my help. Just pretend I'm not even here."

"I can't pretend you're not here because it's all your fault!" she screamed.

"What in the hell are you talking about?" he asked, completely confused.

"You don't give a shit about anyone but yourself. I don't know what the deal is with you and Mason's family or your friends, but I know you're good to them because there is some hidden agenda there."

"I love them!" he retorted.

"You loved Ethan, too, right?" she asked, her voice broken.

"I still do," he answered without hesitation. He was panting even though he had no reason to be breathing so heavily.

"You killed him," she whispered so low Benny wasn't even sure that he had heard her at first.

Benny walked closer to her. But when her head snapped back up, she backed up away from him, her body stopping when she hit the couch behind her.

"Stay away from me!" she screamed.

He reached out to her, wanting to hold her, comfort her, something, like he hadn't allowed himself to do all those years ago. He didn't deserve to touch her, but he needed it himself. She had gotten one thing right – sometimes, his love for his friends felt like the only thing keeping him on this side of the world. He would have given up a long time ago. So yes, it was selfish. But it was also real. He'd gladly give up that hold to this world if it meant happiness for any of the people that he cared about.

"Don't touch me," she yelled.

He couldn't help it. She reminded him so much of the little girl she was – the one he watched with a fascination that he didn't quite understand at the time. He reached out toward her, but she batted his hands away. He dropped them and stood staring at her, watching the silent tears trailing down her cheeks, leaving black marks from her mascara.

"You killed him." She spoke softly, her voice shaking, but the anger in her tone was loud and clear. "You killed him. You killed my baby. You took everything away from me. You think you're a changed man, Benjamin? You think because you have people who care about you now and look up to you that it makes what you did before okay? It doesn't. Ethan cared about you. He looked up to you and you threw him to the wolves. It makes me wonder just how long before it's Mason's turn. Then who? Katy? Benji?

How long before anyone else you love dies? Am I in the line of fire now that I'm back in your life, whether I want to be or not? Are you going to not only take my baby from me, but my life, too?"

Benny was stunned silent. He had known Sophie didn't care for him, but he had assumed it was because of the painful memories he evoked. He never once thought that she blamed him for Ethan's death. He should have known, though. He should have known that she'd know all the ins and outs of his relationship with Ethan, and she'd know the truth – that he really was responsible. It was truly his fault.

He wanted to say something, to retort, to tell her that she was wrong – but she wasn't. Benny always had some smart comment, something to say to twist the situation, but not now. For the first time in years, he was mute.

He didn't know how long he stood in that same position, but he felt the wetness on his own cheeks just as Sophie broke the silence with her whispered words. "Get out."

He looked at her and tried to process her words. "Get out," she repeated louder. He nodded but couldn't move his body. She shoved him, hard. "Get out!" she screamed. "Get the hell out of my house, you murderer! I want you gone, now!"

He was well and truly a murderer, but that was the first time anyone had said it just like that. The words stung, the truth behind them digging a knife straight through his heart. *What could he say?* There were no words. She was right.

"I'm sorry," he whispered, although he knew it wasn't nearly enough. He turned and ran out just as he heard something crash.

It took two bottles of whiskey before he passed out that night, and even then, the dreams haunted him. Ethan and Sophie haunted him.

CHAPTER TEN

Benny practically jumped out of bed when he heard a loud screeching noise. It took him a moment to realize that it was his phone ringing. With the way his head was pounding and his whole body felt like clay that had been molded one too many times, he was tempted to throw it across the room and watch it shatter. He only refrained because he saw that it was Kat calling.

"Kitty Kat, I love you, but you better have a good reason for calling," he groaned, his mouth feeling like he swallowed an entire bag of cotton.

"I would have probably felt like you sound, but Mase took care of me this morning," she chuckled.

"I don't need to know that," he laughed at his own joke and then instantly regretted it when he winced from the pain. He had heard Kat's giggle through the phone before they were both silent for a few moments. "Everything okay?" Benny asked, getting a bit concerned.

"I don't know, Benny. You tell me."

"Well, I could use a hangover cure right about now. Will probably take some meds in a sec, but other than that, yeah, I guess I'm fine."

"Don't bullshit me," she stated flatly. "You never let me lie to myself; guess it's time I repay the favor."

"What are you talking about?" Benny asked, only slightly confused.

"You forget that one, I know you, two, I care about you and want you to be happy, and three, I had drinks with Sophie last night."

"And?" he asked, fishing for information.

"And you need to talk to her, Benny. You need to fix things between you and her."

"She doesn't want to talk to me," he stated, his voice dropping low as the emotions from the night before flooded him.

"It doesn't matter what she wants. Given that I don't remember everything about last night, but I do remember that she said some things that didn't sound like you. She needs to talk to you, and you need to talk to her."

"You weren't there last night when I dropped her off, Kat. She hates me."

"She doesn't hate you; she just has a hard time dealing with her past."

"You mean dealing with me." It wasn't a question.

"No, dealing with the past. I have a feeling that you two have different versions of it, and you need to get your stories straight."

"How much do you know?" He lowered his voice.

"I know enough, and until a few minutes ago, I thought maybe the reason I didn't know about any of this from you was because you had dealt with it and moved on. But, now, I know that you need to deal with your past, too."

"I killed my brother," he whispered it, like he was telling Kat a secret.

"Oh Benny, you didn't kill him. I'm so sorry for your brother, and I'm even sorrier for you. I'm here for you; you know that. Aside from the fact that you were there for me when I needed a friend the most and I owe you so much, I want to help you. Tell me what I can do to help you cope with all this."

"You know all that social work stuff doesn't work on me," Benny replied, trying to lighten the mood.

"It's not social work, and it does work," she huffed. Benny laughed. "Hey! I know what you're trying to do. No distracting me."

"How do you manage to keep your kids in order?" he chuckled.

"I've had a lot of practice between you and Mason," she added dryly. "Seriously, though, Benny, you need to talk to someone about this. I'm all ears, and I'll do my best to get you to see yourself the way that I see you, but I feel like the best medicine for both you and Sophie is to deal with this together. You share some of the same pain, the same resentment. If you can talk things through, you can both get closure. Don't you think that your brother would want that for the two people he loved the most?"

"Low blow, Kitty Kat," Benny sighed. "I can't. You didn't see the look in Sophie's eyes last night. And she's right, you know?"

"She's not. You're not. And *you* didn't see the look in her eyes when she told me the story. And on that note, every story has two sides. And I think hers might be a little skewed. Since I only heard hers, you feel like telling me yours?"

"Not today."

"Fine, fair enough. But go talk to Sophie, make her understand."

"What is there to understand? She's got all the facts right."

"I'm pretty sure she doesn't; there are things she probably doesn't know. And there are things you should know about as well."

"Like what?"

"Not my story to tell, Benny. But go talk to her. Go try to make things right between you two."

"I'll think about it."

"I'm not getting off the phone until you agree."

"You know that I'd never hang up on you, but I'm not above putting the phone down and going about my life, especially right now. Come on, Kat, my head is killing me and I can't do this right now."

"I'm not giving up."

"Fine, but drop it for now, yeah?"

"Yeah, all right. Go take some aspirin and feel better."

"Thanks."

They hung up and Benny shuffled out of bed to get himself some food, water, and pills. It had taken another hour before he felt a little more like himself. It was only then that he allowed Kat's words to sink in. He did have the urge to talk to Sophie, to get her to listen to him, but he wasn't sure what he would say. *I'm sorry I killed my brother and hurt us both in the process?*

There was no way he could talk to her, no matter what Kat said.

CHAPTER ELEVEN

Sophie should have known drinking those stupid fruity drinks would be a bad idea. With shots, she knew just how many she could drink before she started to have loose lips, but with the interesting concoctions that Kat had convinced her to drink, she couldn't taste the alcohol. Before she knew what she was doing, she was spilling her whole life's story to Kat, who was probably even drunker than Sophie. When Sophie woke up with a splitting headache and flashes of a heated argument with Benny, she had high hopes that Kat wouldn't remember much. That notion was quickly dashed the following day.

"Look, Sophie, I didn't know Benny at that time in his life, but I know him now and he was my rock during some pretty bad times in my life," Kat started in on Sophie when she called to "check on her" the next day. Sophie wasn't even sure how talking of never drinking again turned into a conversation about Benny.

"I know you mean well, Kat, but I'm asking you to drop this subject. I've never told anyone about what happened, and no offense, but I'd like to pretend that I didn't tell you either."

"That's not healthy. You need to talk to someone. And who better than the only other person you know who's been suffering the same way?"

"What?" Sophie screeched.

"I think you should give Benny a chance to tell his side of the story."

"I don't need his side. I was there, living it every damn day."

"Okay, okay," she could hear Kat backtracking, "it's just that…well, maybe you misunderstood things between him and Ethan. Benny would never encourage him to join a gang or help him or whatever else you thought you heard; he would never lead the people he loves astray."

"I know what I heard," Sophie argued.

"And maybe you heard wrong. Look, all I'm saying is that fine, sure, maybe Benny wasn't who he was then, but you've seen him now. He's kind and caring, and most importantly, he always puts others' needs above his own. He couldn't have been all that much different from who he is now."

"He didn't use to."

"Okay, fine," Kat conceded, "I didn't know him then, so maybe he didn't, but you can't believe that people won't ever change?"

"It doesn't change the past, even if he's not the same guy he used to be."

"Maybe it does, maybe it's not supposed to. Maybe you're supposed to grow and evolve with it. All I know is that as happy and carefree as Benny may seem to the world, there is a lingering sadness. There has always been that pain just under the surface. He's not the kind of guy you push for answers, but now I get what it's all about. If he was a monster then, he wouldn't feel that way."

"He's a thug!" Sophie cried out, trying to find something to retort with, not liking how Kat's conversation was making her feel.

"Ex-thug," Kat pointed out.

"Once a thug, always a thug."

"I suppose you're going to say once a convict always a convict, too?" Sophie knew she was referring to Mason. He had been upfront about what happened to him, and that was actually what had drawn Sophie to his office rather than the other two she had interviewed at.

"He was never supposed to be a convict," Sophie stated. "Benny was always a thug."

"Well, now you're just insulting me. He is the godfather of my children, after all. You think I'd let someone who I don't trust with my life have that kind of responsibility."

"Kat, I'm sorry, I didn't mean it that way. It's just…after everything that I told you, how can you possibly think that I even want to think about Benny, let alone talk to him?"

"I'm not going to pretend that I know all the details, but if I know Benny, then it wasn't his fault."

"It was," Sophie stated dryly.

"Then I'm at fault for putting Mason in jail."

"Huh?"

"I know Mason told you all about his stint in prison, but what exactly do you know?"

"That he was falsely accused of rape and spent time in prison until evidence came to light afterward that cleared his name and overturned his conviction."

"Right, well, that's all true, but what you don't know is that it was my twin sister who accused him."

Sophie gasped loudly. "I don't understand."

"It's not really something that we go around telling people, so I'd appreciate it if you didn't air out our dirty laundry, but I was in foster care all my life. I didn't know that I had a twin. She had been the one to accuse

Mason, and without going into all the details, it was because of that situation that Mason and I met."

"But…I don't…where is your sister now?"

"She passed away," Kat said, her voice shaking a bit.

"I'm sorry."

"Me, too, but the point is that she accused Mason, not me."

"Okay…" Sophie drew out the word.

"But maybe things would have turned out differently if I had taken more interest in the family that I came from. I could have researched, maybe even found her, and then she would have turned out differently and presto, no false accusation."

"How does that relate to Benny?"

"In a few ways, actually. Do you honestly believe that if Benny knew what the outcome of his actions would be that he would have stayed on that path? Because let me tell you, if I had known that I had a sister out there who was spiraling downward, I would have found her. Next, as much as I hate admitting this…but if my sister hadn't done what she did, I wouldn't have met Mason. And if you were to ask him, he'd agree, but please don't ask him. I really don't want him thinking about that time again. And lastly, do you know who helped Mason deal with everything he went through in prison and then after? Who stood by him when plenty of other people didn't? Who looked after me when I needed someone's shoulder? Who made sure I was okay when no one else cared? Who is solely responsible for helping Mason and I get our heads out of our asses to find happiness together? I could go on, Sophie, but I'm sure you see where I'm going with this. Through everything we went through, we leaned on Benny. Why? What was his incentive? Love, Sophie. That was his motivation. He loves us, and when he loves someone, he takes care of them. Sometimes things happen outside of our control, things we wish we could go back and fix, but that doesn't change how strongly we love the people who matter the most to us. And when things go sour, we die a little inside, especially if we feel responsible. Trust me; I've lived through that. Believe me when I say that Benny isn't the monster you think he is."

"I don't think he's a monster," Sophie whispered. That wasn't entirely true. Sometimes, she did think he was a monster, but with Kat's words echoing through her head, he wasn't.

"That's a good start."

"I…uh…I have to go, Kat. Thanks for checking on me."

"Sure."

Sophie couldn't handle the emotions that were overwhelming her with the direction the conversation had taken. She had seen firsthand glimpses of not only the man Benny used to be before he joined the gang, the good side of him, but also moments where he had matured, become something bigger and better. Yet, those were easy to push back. Not so much when Kat put it in her face. She didn't like that…she didn't like it one bit. She especially hated the nagging voice that said maybe Kat was right; maybe whatever little tidbits she had heard between Ethan and Benny had been misconstrued in her head. Maybe, she hated to admit, that she used that as a way to blame Benny first for the decline in her and Ethan's relationship because she wouldn't blame Ethan. Later, she held onto it to blame Benny for Ethan's death, the loss of her baby, because she needed somewhere to point all her emotions toward so she could move on. It was easy to say Benny was the cause because she had heard him pushing Ethan to join a gang. In her young mind, she could have easily made the words bigger than they were, imagining that Benny was forcing Ethan into it. With time, memories became skewed, hatred evolved, pain increased, and that was where she was at – bitter and alone despite all her outward accomplishments.

She curled up on her sofa, a warm blanket covering her from head to toe even though it was warm in her place. She needed the comfort; she needed something to stop the trembling she was experiencing. She watched romantic comedy after romantic comedy until her eyes burned and she fell asleep.

CHAPTER TWELVE

Kat had kept her promise and worked on Benny to contact Sophie. He didn't want to, he really didn't want to, but it was hard to say no to Kat. He told her it wasn't a good idea; he told her that he didn't know what to say; he even told her that he'd think about it, but she had a knack for wearing people down. She wasn't the backing down kind. Even while she was essentially Mason's slave, she hadn't lost her will to keep going and make the best of the life she was living. It was no wonder that she was trying to push that onto Benny as well.

It took about a month until he finally relented and told Kat that he'd give Sophie a call to see if they could talk about their shared past. It took another day for him to figure out just what he'd say to her, but that had all been for nothing because Sophie didn't answer his call. She didn't pick up when he called her the next day or the following day, either. And she didn't return his call when he finally left a very simple message on her phone on the fourth day.

"Hi Sophie, it's Benny. I'd really like to talk to you. Please give me a call."

"Are you sure that you have the right number?" Kat asked him when she checked for about the millionth time to see if he called.

"Yeah, Kitty Kat, I'm sure. The voicemail is her voice and it says something like, 'You've reached Dr. Sophie Basi.'"

"Try again."

"I told you this was a bad idea," he responded.

"But she seemed so receptive," Kat mumbled so low that Benny barely caught it. He was about to ask Kat what in the hell that meant when she changed the subject. "Okay, how about dinner tomorrow?"

"What?" Kat was a ball of energy when she had to be, but that was a quick change, even for her.

"I haven't had some grown-up time in a while, and when you've come over lately, you and Mason stick me with the kids. I'll get a babysitter and the three of us can go out and catch up. I need a break and you need to clear your head. You busy tomorrow?"

"Nope, not busy. Sounds like fun. You sure Mason is free?"

"Yeah, I just checked his schedule."

"Sounds good. You can probably get John to babysit if he's not busy. You know those kids have him wrapped around their fingers."

He heard Kat's giggle through the phone before they made plans and said their goodbyes.

*****

Benny made his way into the restaurant where he was meeting Kat and Mason. After the hostess led him to the table, he noticed Kat sitting alone.

"Where's Mason?"

"Oh, he's around," she responded vaguely as he hugged her. She seemed to brighten up as they pulled apart. "There you are!" she exclaimed at whoever was behind Benny.

He turned to find a wide-eyed Sophie gaping at him. Kat pulled a stunned Sophie into a quick embrace before she turned to both of them.

"Well, if you haven't figured it out already, this is a set-up. If you don't sit down and enjoy a nice meal together and at least be civil with each other, I will have to use more drastic measures next time. And you both know that I mean it. So go on, enjoy. I'm out."

They stared at each other in awkward silence for a few beats before Benny finally laughed at the absurdity of the situation.

"I think we've been had."

That brought a smile to Sophie's lips. "You know she means it when she says that she'll pull something crazier next time."

"Oh, I know," he chuckled before getting more serious. He pulled a chair out for Sophie as he said, "So, shall we?"

"I guess."

"So enthusiastic," he tried to tease, but Sophie just gave him a tight smile. He sat and faced her. "Listen, I'm sorry for all this. I had no idea and if you want to leave, feel free. I'll even tell Kat that you stayed all night and it was great and she can stop meddling."

"No, no, it's fine. She went through the trouble."

"You have no idea," Benny added.

"I'm pretty sure I do. She can talk someone's ear off." Sophie smiled.

"Only when it's something that she thinks is important."

"I guess that's meant to be a compliment?" Sophie asked.

"Sort of." The silence came back. "I tried calling you."

"Yeah, I was busy."

"Not trying to avoid me?"

"I was busy trying to avoid you," Sophie teased, a smile forming on her lips.

"About that night," Benny started.

"No," Sophie cut him off. "Let's not, okay? We're at dinner at a nice place. I don't want to make a scene, and I really don't want to rehash that night or the memories it leads to. So, let's just have a nice dinner and leave all the other stuff behind."

"That sounds good to me," Benny responded, more than willing to steer clear of anything having to do with his role in Ethan's death.

Sophie suddenly chuckled low. "What's funny?" Benny asked.

"When I first saw you, I thought it was the worst thing to happen to me in a while. After getting my bearings down, I figured I'd see you at most once a year thanks to our association with Kat and Mason. And here I am, seeing you at least once a month, instead."

Benny couldn't help but laugh, too. "Honestly, Sophie, I figured I'd rarely see you, too."

"It's always like that, huh? When you need something to happen, it doesn't, but when you don't need it to, it does."

"Always."

The evening progressed wonderfully from there. They ate, talked, and more importantly, they laughed as if they were on a fantastic first date. The girl with the keen eye and the inquisitive streak was back in full force, and it took all Benny had to fight the urge to allow the feelings of fascination he had for her spring back to the surface. She was the same girl that he used to know and yet, she was different. Life, experience, even age had changed her from a scrawny but interesting girl to an intelligent, beautiful woman. It was over the course of that two-hour "date" that Benny stopped looking at Sophie as a reminder of Ethan and what he had lost. Instead, he looked at her like a painting in a museum – mysterious, otherworldly, stunning, and unattainable. She was no longer Ethan's Sophie in Benny's mind. She was just Sophie.

They argued, they agreed, they even got a bit heated when they discussed the computer system Benny had set up in Mason's office for his birthday. They didn't, however, discuss Ethan, and Benny was fine with that.

It had been a very pleasant evening when they finally left the restaurant.

"I'll follow you home," Benny announced as they made their way to the parking lot.

"Oh, that's not necessary," Sophie told him.

"I know, but I want to make sure you get home safe, and I have nothing else to do."

"Well, when you put it that way," she responded dryly, but with a smile on her face.

Benny knew where she lived, but he still followed her car to her home. He parked, got out, and leaned against the side of his car as he watched her walk to her door.

"I'm home safe," she called out as she waved at him. He wanted to walk up to her, show her inside, watch her walk through her door, but this wasn't a date. He had been thanking his lucky stars for how the evening had gone already; he wasn't going to push it.

Apparently, someone thought he hadn't had enough luck because he watched her trip over her heels. Not that the near miss was lucky but having an excuse to rush forward and steady her was.

"You okay?" he asked sincerely, keeping an arm around her waist.

"Yeah, I'm fine. Thanks," she seemed to choke out.

Benny led her to her door where she fumbled in her purse to find the key. She tried to put the key in the lock but was having trouble.

"Here, let me," Benny offered, his hand skimming along hers, the warmth of her skin tingling his own. As he reached the key, she turned toward him. Her eyes were alight with mischief, their warm brown color so inviting, so alluring. He could feel his own lips part as he was caught in her mesmerizing gaze. She probably didn't even know what she did to him. He told himself that he should walk away, but he couldn't. He didn't want to.

Before he could stop himself, he leaned forward, closing the distance between them as his lips brushed hers lightly. He could taste a lingering hint of the wine that she had been sipping, and it was almost as intoxicating as the feel of her lips touching his. It was no more than a peck, a simple contact, but it was like nothing Benny had ever felt. They stayed like that, their lips whispering with each other for mere seconds before Sophie pulled away.

He looked up into her eyes, no longer pulsing with fire, but rather with confusion clouding the deep brown color. It burned him.

"I'm sorry, Sophie. I shouldn't have done that." She didn't respond, only stared at him. "I should go," he started and turned to walk away. Try as he might, he couldn't. He took no more than two steps before he turned and grabbed Sophie in his arms, his lips seeking hers. She gasped at the contact, which allowed his tongue to find the entrance into her mouth. She hesitated for a moment and then her tongue danced with his. If he thought the peck was something to write home about, this was something to show up at your parents' doorstep with a new wife and kid on the way. He held her close while he felt her hands burrow into his shirt, pulling him closer. It felt incredible. It was the thing in his life that he hadn't realized was missing. And then it was over, just like that, as she pulled away...no, more like forced her body from his.

Her hand came up to cover her mouth, tears instantly streaked down her face and he could hear her breathing heavily as she mumbled, "Oh, my God."

"Sophie." He spoke her name as if it was a prayer. He reached for her, but she stepped back and bent at the waist, her tears now breaking into sobs as her other hand dropped the purse she was holding and grabbed at her stomach.

"Sophie," he tried again.

"Don't touch me," she said loudly as her head snapped up.

"I'm so sorry. I was out of line."

"You kissed me," she hissed as if Benny had committed some unspeakable crime.

"I shouldn't have," he answered.

"I kissed you." Her tone was flat with a hint of surprise.

"Let me just make sure you get inside okay and I'll go."

"I kissed a murderer." It was as if she was talking to herself, her thoughts forming words instead of quiet revelations in her head. Benny felt those words through to his very core.

"Sophie, I'm so sorry," he told her but wasn't sure what good that would do or what exactly he was sorry for.

"I can't believe I kissed you." She finally looked at him, her voice full of venom. "You took him from me and I kissed you." Benny was hurting from Ethan's death as it was. He felt responsible and it killed him to know that Sophie felt that way, too. And yet, competing with a ghost stung the worst. "You killed my baby!" she screamed.

"You're right," he responded, defeated. "I loved Ethan and I didn't protect him. I caused his murder. I might as well have pulled the trigger. You're right to hate me, but please don't do this. Please don't be upset with yourself." He hated seeing her this way. He just needed her to see this was yet another thing to add to his list of crimes. This wasn't her fault and she couldn't beat herself up about it. He had kissed her and she was just caught in the moment. He told her as much. "You didn't have a choice. I kissed you."

She nodded as if she agreed with Benny, but he could see the wheels turning in her head. "I heard you and Ethan talking," she told him. "I heard you encouraging him to join with you. I heard you telling him that you'd help. You did, and it got him killed. You led him straight into the lion's den. It wasn't enough that you were playing Russian roulette with your life, you had to force it on Ethan?"

"What?" Benny gasped. "Never," he added vehemently.

"But I heard you!" she practically whined.

"Whatever you think you heard, Sophie, I swear on all I hold dear that I never encouraged Ethan. I *dis*-couraged him. I did everything I could to make sure that he didn't follow my path. I knew what I had gotten into, but it was too late for me. I never wanted that for Ethan. I made sure that he knew that. I threatened him, I warned him off, I did everything but watch him twenty-four-seven, and that's where I failed him. You're right when you say that I'm responsible, but it's because I didn't protect him, not because I led him."

Sophie stared at him, her brows creased, her eyes watery, but he swore he saw relief pass her features, like she was hoping that's what he was going to say. "Kat was right," she mumbled so low he had to strain to hear her words.

He saw her take several deep breaths before she steeled her spine and looked Benny in the eye. "It doesn't change the fact that Ethan is gone. He died following your footsteps. And it doesn't change the fact that my baby is gone and I didn't get a chance to tell him."

"Tell him what?" he asked, truly confused.

"My baby. Our baby...Ethan's child..." she trailed off, the sobs returning full force as she hugged her stomach.

"Oh, God, no," Benny whispered, the impact and the meaning of her words sinking in.

"Oh yes," she cried. "I found out the day that he was murdered. The stress of his death put too much of a toll on my body. I miscarried a month later." She had stepped closer and her pain was apparent, each word punctuated as if it were a separate sentence.

"My baby is gone. And Ethan never even knew that he was going to be a father."

Benny had considered himself strong, definitely tough, but at this instant, he felt like a weak man, a shell of himself. He didn't know when it happened, but he found himself kneeling on the floor in front of Sophie, as if he was in a church, begging for forgiveness. Maybe he was. He tasted the salt on his lips from the tears trailing down his cheeks.

"Leave, Benny," Sophie stated with dead calm, only the tiny hitch in her voice giving away her pain. "Get up and get the hell out of here." He didn't want to leave her, didn't want to have her go through the pain all over again by herself if he could be there for her this time.

"Sophie, Sophie, I'm so sorry. I don't....I didn't..." He couldn't find the words.

"Your sorry isn't welcome here."

"I can't...I..."

"I said get up and get the hell out of here." She spoke louder this time, her voice sounding constricted. He tried to oblige, not sure what else to do, but his legs wouldn't comply. He looked up at her, his eyes begging for her strength because right then, she had it all and he had none.

"You don't get it, do you?" she gritted. "He never knew that he was going to be a father. And yeah, we were young, but he would have been a fantastic dad." She paused as if she was collecting her thoughts. "When

Ethan died, a little part of me died with him, but with his child growing in me, it made up for that missing piece. I still had Ethan with me. He was going to live on, but my body couldn't handle the initial grief, and I lost the last part of Ethan. Do you get it now? I lost him twice," she whispered. "I lost Ethan twice. I couldn't manage it then, and I doubt that I can do it now." Her voice was faraway like she was reliving the moment all over again. It broke Benny's heart just listening to her.

"I'm sorry," Benny whispered.

Sophie narrowed her eyes, no longer in an explaining mode. "I told you that your sorrys are no good here. Words, Benny, they're just words. You want to show me your actions?" Benny nodded. "Then for once, do as you're told and get the fuck out of here. Let me live my misery in peace." Her voice was no longer shrill, no longer angry. It was crushed. That cut deeper than anything Benny had ever experienced. He was powerless to do anything but listen to her plea.

He stood slowly, the tears still burning his cheeks. He tipped his head at Sophie as if in surrender before turning on his heel and walking away. He made it to John's place, unsure how he even got there, and proceeded to cry with the only other person who would truly understand his pain.

CHAPTER THIRTEEN

All Benny wanted to do for the next month was drink until he was numb and stay holed up at his place…alone. After leaving John's the night that he found out about Sophie and Ethan's baby, he managed to stay under the radar for a few days. John came and checked on him numerous times, as did Chain, but he shooed them away. Chain hadn't stood a chance against drunken Benny, and John was surrounded by his own pain.

He blew off calls from Kat and Mason several times as well. He wasn't in the mood to talk to anyone. No, he didn't deserve to talk to anyone. He deserved the death that was Ethan's and his unborn child. *Why him?* he wondered. Why was it Ethan who had to die instead of him? If Ethan were still alive, he'd have done something wonderful with his life, unlike Benny. He'd have married Sophie, and they'd have a family together. His parents would still have a son, and everyone would be happy. Nothing would be amiss if Benny was six feet under. Life would go on as usual. Instead, the world was a mess, his brother was long dead, the woman he had feelings for hated him, rightly so, and he was a baby killer.

"I would have been an uncle," he mused aloud. "Sophie would have been a mom," he said to the empty space. "She would have been a wonderful mom. And all her son's friends would have had crushes on her." He smiled, the only happy thought to enter his head in the past few days.

"I seem to recall you getting mad at me for doing the same." He had heard Mason's voice before he saw him.

"Go away," Benny slurred.

"Sorry, buddy, but you were there for me when I needed you, and I'll be there for you when you need me."

"This is different," Benny whined. He actually whined.

"Give me this." Mason pulled the bottle of vodka out of Benny's hand. "You look like shit, you smell even worse, and everyone is worried about you. This isn't you. Me, I can understand. Maybe even John," Mason chuckled at his own joke, "but not you. You're the guy who stops assholes like us from sulking."

"I'm not sulking."

"Then what do you call it?"

"Self-medicating."

"Yeah, not so much," Mason told him.

"I don't need your help."

"Seems to me like you do."

"How did you know I was here?"

"Well, aside from John and Chain letting me know, I took a guess."

"Good for you. You saw me, you know I'm okay, you can leave now."

"You're far from okay, Benny." He paused. "Look, I know it has something to do with Sophie, but I don't know what."

"How do you know that?"

"Well, Kat told me that she tried to set you and Sophie up. Then the next day, Sophie asked for some personal time. You disappeared at the same time, ignoring all my and Kat's calls. And lastly, John and Chain told me that you were in a bad place and they couldn't snap you out of it. They might have mentioned Sophie's name."

"Traitors," Benny hissed.

"Nope, more accurately, they're friends," Mason told him. "Benny, Kat feels horrible. She feels like it's all her fault, whatever is going on between you two."

"It's not, it's all mine."

"Then you've got to snap out of this to at least tell her that."

"You tell her."

"Come on, Benny, this isn't you. I don't know what happened, and I'm not going to push you to tell me, but we can figure this all out. That's something you taught me, and I'm giving it right back."

"This can't be figured out," Benny declared.

"Why's that?"

"Because I killed Sophie's baby."

"You two slept together?" Mason asked, completely surprised.

"Not mine, my brother's."

"You mentioned him once, but never again. You never talk about him Benny. What's going on there?"

"He's dead," Benny's voice cracked.

"I'm so sorry."

"Don't be, it's all because of me. I'm the sorry one."

"I don't buy that. Tell me what happened."

Benny gave him the story, all of it, even up to the part of the pseudo-date with Sophie and the big reveal.

"I'm real sorry, buddy, for everything you've been through. But explain to me please how any of it was your fault."

"I should have protected Ethan! Sophie lost the baby because of the stress of Ethan's death…a death that I should have prevented. I didn't just ruin one life. Ethan's death wasn't enough. No…I destroyed Sophie as a result, too."

"And maybe he would have died in a car accident a few weeks later, and Sophie would have still lost the baby from grief, and none of this would have mattered. I believe when it's your time to go, you go." Mason paused to let the words sink in. "Look, you know I was the biggest proponent of 'what ifs,' but I'm living proof that sometimes life has to fall apart before it gets to the point where it's supposed to be. Where would you be right now? Probably not here. I'd have died in prison, never met Kat, or find my happily ever after with her, and there'd be no Benji or Katy. Sounds like a horrible life to me. I'm sorry you lost your brother. I know what it's like to lose, and I don't wish that on anyone, but from the ruins of that tragedy, a new life emerged, and I'm thankful for that life. I'm thankful to have *you* in my life."

"Anyone ever tell you that you talk too much?" Benny asked, trying to lighten the mood, but his voice was thick with emotion, tears threatening to fall. Mason had really gotten to him. He wasn't sure if it was the words he used, the threat of not having Mason and his family in his life, or the fact that when he looked at Mason, he saw traces of Ethan. But it all penetrated, even through his alcohol-filled mind.

"I think you might have told me a time or two," Mason laughed. "Let's get you clean and sober and then we can figure out the next steps."

Benny's movements were sluggish, but he managed to shower, eat something, and down coffee with a couple Alka-Seltzers.

"How's Sophie doing?" Benny finally found the courage to ask.

"Kat's spoken to her a few times, and it sounds like she's upset, but all right. I think my wife knows more than she is letting on."

"You watch out for her. She's sneaky," Benny teased, feeling slightly lighter than he did before, but it was still tense. "What do I do about Sophie?" Benny asked on a pained sigh.

"What do you want to do? And more importantly, why? Because you feel guilty? If that's the case, you have nothing to feel guilty about. Her anger and her pain are misplaced. That's on her, and you don't owe her anything. If it's because you don't want things to be weird for Kat and me, you don't have to worry about that. You come first, and besides, you know that Kat doesn't care about awkward situations. And I think that I lost the right to care about that a long time ago, too. If it's because you're sympathetic to her or because you care about her, either as a friend or as more, well, then, you might want to see if you can patch things up between you two."

"I'm still not sober enough for this. You sound like a shrink," Benny told Mason honestly.

"Dr. Tredwell at your services."

"You're not that kind of doctor, wiseass."

"I can still prescribe you the same meds as a psychiatrist."

"Yeah, yeah. When's Eddie going to be done with school? I'd rather go to him for meds. He won't talk my ear off."

"Stop trying to avoid the subject. You're the one who asked about Sophie."

"I didn't expect a two-page answer."

"Then what did you expect?" Mason huffed.

"For you to tell me what to do."

"I recall asking you for advice with Kat."

"I recall several times that you also didn't, even though you should have."

"Why do you keep pulling us off track?" Mason asked sincerely.

"Because I'm afraid of the answer to my own question. What can I do? I can apologize, but what good would that do? She'll still blame me."

"I don't think that she blames you. She's just having a hard time processing everything now that it's back in her face. And you're a painful reminder. Besides, it wasn't your fault," Mason declared.

"Maybe it was, maybe it wasn't. Let's say it wasn't, and I apologize, then I'm admitting I *am* to blame. Still at square one."

"Then try to explain things to her the way I did with you."

"It's easier to listen to an outsider, Mase. I barely believe you even though your life is confirmation that everything you said is true. Sophie isn't going to hear me out if I say the same things to her."

"I can talk to her."

"You don't need to get involved. And she might not listen simply because she thinks you're on my side."

"I *am* on your side, but that doesn't mean that I don't see things clearly."

"What do I do?"

"Show her that you care about Ethan's loss and that baby's loss just as much as she does. She can't see how much this is affecting you the way your friends can."

"So what? Show up at her house in tears?" he asked sarcastically.

"Yeah, don't think that will work," Mason snorted. "You once told me I had to fight for Kat. Well, consider this your version of fighting for Sophie."

"We're not in love, Mase. We're not a couple. We're not even friends. There's nothing to fight for."

"We'll debate about the love part later," Mason said very quickly before adding, "You care about her. That's all that matters."

"Okay, so then what?"

"When I fought for Kat, I did something that was meaningful to both of us. It was a risk, but if it worked out in my favor, it would be something we'd both understand and appreciate. As you know, it worked."

"Show her I care. Show her I care," Benny repeated. Then it hit him. "Something meaningful to us both," he said with a slight smile.

"You got an idea?"

"Yeah, Mase, I think I do."

"Good."

"Thanks for…well, everything, friend."

"It's brother," Mason responded. At Benny's curious stare, he added. "It's 'thanks, brother,' not 'friend.' We're not blood, Benny, but sometimes family is chosen, and you're the family I chose. So, thank *you*, brother."

"I love you, *bro*," Benny pulled Mason into a hug as he emphasized "bro."

"Love you, too, Benny. Love you, too."

CHAPTER FOURTEEN

Sophie had needed some personal time after reliving all the painful memories she had pushed down. She had tried to stay strong when she told Benny all about her unborn child, but it was no use. Her emotions had overwhelmed her. One minute she was having thoughts about Benny that she had no business thinking, then he was kissing her, and God help her, but she had wanted it. She had liked it, though "like" wasn't even a strong enough word. The initial shock of Benny's kiss had quickly dissipated as she welcomed the warm feel of his lips. It was mere seconds only, but as her mind fought her body, she realized what she did, and more importantly, who she had done it with.

The pain and anger she felt over losing Ethan and then losing the remaining part of him was something she never fully grieved. It had felt like she lost Ethan twice, and she just couldn't deal with it then, so she placed all her emotions in a box in her mind. When Benny came back into her life, everything she had fought so hard to keep locked away had surfaced. It was like Ethan had died just yesterday, and the feelings she had toward Benny came back, too. Only, the Benny she knew now wasn't the Benny that she remembered from then. It was hard for her to differentiate the two, and in that moment, the past won out.

As much as she wanted Benny to leave her, she wanted him to fight her – to stay and comfort her – because God knows, she never truly got that. Her parents had never really been there for her. God help them, they tried, but they just weren't great with emotions. They offered to pay for a shrink, but when Sophie declined, they felt their emotional obligations had been met. She stayed away from her home a lot at that time because her grief seemed to make them uncomfortable. She spent time with her friends, and they were there for her, but they didn't know what it was like. They hadn't experienced the kind of loss she had. As much as she hated Benny and blamed him – although, that blame had taken a huge beating after he confirmed what she was starting to suspect. Even though she still thought of him as a selfish bastard for whatever part he did play in Ethan's death, a very deep part of her believed that he would understand what she went through. But the lingering anger and the deep-seated pain were tipping the scales against Benny. When he finally left her in peace, she was both relieved and upset.

Aside from history overpowering her very being, it was the confusion she felt over the very person whom she vowed to hate that had tied her in knots. She wanted to slap him and beg him to hold her at the same time. She called Mason and asked for some days off to get her head back on straight. He obliged, but days turned into weeks, and then suddenly it was a month of self-loathing, crying, reliving memories, watching sad movies, some more crying, talking to herself aloud, barely eating, and then more crying.

She avoided Kat's calls for about two weeks, but when that woman had something on her mind, clearly no one stood a chance. She started showing up. At first, she'd just sit with Sophie and watch TV, obviously realizing that Sophie just needed the company. Sometimes she made food, other times just tea or coffee. She brought Benji and Katy a couple of times. It hurt Sophie's heart, but it also lightened it, too. Strange how you could have two warring emotions at the same time. It had been a little over a month when Kat finally said, "Sophie, we need to talk."

"Are you breaking up with me?" Sophie tried to joke, but Kat didn't look amused.

"You're miserable, Sophie, and I hate seeing you this way."

"Does Mason need me back at work?"

"No…I mean, he always needs you, but you can take all the time in the world to sort out your problems. I just don't think it's healthy."

"Who are you to judge?" Sophie snapped. Kat looked hurt and Sophie immediately backpedaled. "Sorry. I didn't mean that. You've been nothing but kind to me…better than my other friends, actually."

"No, I get it. I was the opposite. When I was in a shitty situation, I wanted someone to talk to if only to talk. I'm just trying to be there for you, Sophie. I didn't go through what you did, but I know what a shitty life looks like. I know struggling, I know about finding joy out of misery, I know loss, and more importantly, I know love."

"I get that, I do, but I just don't even understand myself right now."

"Maybe I can try to help," Kat offered. "Why don't you start by telling me what's bothering you."

"Where do I even begin?"

"Wherever you need to."

"Well, you know about my past with Benny, right?"

"Yeah, and I know that whether he was to blame or not, people change. I'm sure you've seen it."

"I have," Sophie admitted quietly. "But, see, that's the thing. My mind might recognize that Benny isn't really to blame. I mean, I heard your words; I heard his, and I was wrong about thinking that he pushed Ethan, but that still doesn't change the fact that Ethan did follow him for his approval and Benny knew that before he went in. Not to mention that I realize he's not the person he once was, I can see that he's a changed man, but being around him is putting me right back into the past. The guy from my perception – the one who took everyone I loved from me is overlapping with the guy he is now. How do I differentiate between the two? How do I get my mind to comprehend everything and forgive him, forgive Ethan, even forgive myself, for all our prior sins because no matter what, we all played a role in the past?"

"I have to preface this by saying I'm not demeaning what happened to you, but let me ask you this, what would have happened if Ethan were still here?"

"I'm guessing we'd be married with kids."

"That's just it, you're guessing. You might have broken up, drifted apart, or you might have been blissfully happy."

"But we'll never know."

"Exactly, so why dwell on what you don't know? Why let it break your heart over and over?"

"But we didn't drift apart; he was taken from me. It's not like we went through the natural curve of highs and lows in a relationship. It's not like we broke up. We were at the top of the mountain."

"Were you really? You didn't have any issues? You didn't resent the time that he took away from you?"

"Oh God, I'm a horrible person because I did, and I do," Sophie put her face in her hands as the tears ran down her face. "Why wasn't I enough?" she mumbled from behind her hands. "God, I hated him for that. Even after he died, I hated him. I wanted to blame him, tell him that it was his own doing, but how could I do that to someone who was gone? He couldn't defend himself against my hatred."

"That's one of the stages of grief, Sophie. It's completely natural and healthy for you to have done that. But you felt guilty, right?" Kat asked as she stroked Sophie's back, trying to comfort her. Sophie simply nodded, her face still in her hands. "Do you think that maybe you channeled that hatred and blame to Benny because you felt like you couldn't blame Ethan?"

"No," Sophie said as she straightened up. "Benny knew Ethan would follow his every footstep. Ethan looked up to him. Heck, I looked up to him. I always loved Ethan, but Benny was this force, this almost otherworldly person who you couldn't help but look at in awe. And Ethan was his little brother. Of course, he was going to try to be like Benny." She paused and breathed in deeply. "And now, I'm not sure what to think. He didn't push Ethan. He said he tried to stop him, and I do believe him. I'm oddly thankful for that." She meant it. It was nice to know that Ethan had Benny in his corner even when she thought he hadn't been. "Even with all that, Benny knew that Ethan would want to be just like him and he didn't care because if he did, he'd have stopped his lifestyle before he even started it."

"How old was Benny then?"

"In his twenties."

"Do you remember being in your twenties?"

"Yes," Sophie responded.

"And how often did you think about the consequences of your actions toward others? I mean, you lived through something big, so you were probably more in tune with ramifications than others were, but even little things like flirting with some guy you weren't going to hook up with – did you worry about sending him the wrong signals? I'll bet no. And like I said, you were probably a special case, but think of all the other people your age then. Did they have any cares in the world?"

"But this was different," Sophie cried.

"I don't really see how this is different, except that maybe the outcome was horrific, but most terrible results aren't expected. Let's say for argument's sake that this situation is different and Benny is wholeheartedly to blame. Do you honestly think that Benny wanted Ethan to die? That he wanted to lose his brother and everything he held dear? Do you think it didn't affect him? That he wasn't in pain? Maybe he grieved differently than you, but he's allowed to grieve however he sees fit. All I know is that I hated my sister when she killed herself, and yet, there was still a part of me that was upset she was gone. If I felt that way over her, imagine what Benny felt over Ethan."

"You're not allowed to make sense right now," Sophie told Kat between tears. Kat hadn't said anything that Sophie hadn't already secretly thought about before; she just could never admit it out loud. Having Kat force her to speak about it made it real, made all the feelings she had on the subject mean something more than just anguish.

"I just want you to be happy, Sophie, and clearly, this is eating away at you. I don't know if it's the pain being fresh or your conflicting feelings about Benny, but I do know that he's miserable, too. I don't expect you to work things out overnight...I know, I know." Kat put her hands up in defense, "I thought it might work that way before, but I was wrong. All I'm saying is that the first step to healing is forgiving. You can't do that on your own and neither can Benny. Be there for each other, help each other. No one understands this grief better than you two."

"Why do you care?" Sophie asked, part of her knowing Kat genuinely wanted Sophie to bury the past, but a stronger part of her figured that it was for Benny's sake.

"Because I don't like seeing you like this."

"It has nothing to do with Benny?"

"I love Benny like a brother. I want to see him happy so badly that it hurts, and this is affecting him just as strongly as it's affecting you. Of course, I want it all to work out, and I really think you both can benefit from mourning together, but that has nothing to do with why I want to see you smile."

"Why does it matter if I figure this out with Benny or without him?"

"Because I think the reason this is still affecting you so strong is because you never got proper closure. You needed something from Benny back then, some comfort, some explanation maybe, that you never got. If you guys can work things out, then maybe you can move past this."

"I...I just...I don't think that I can. The last time I saw him...I was horrible to him."

"He's in a bad place right now himself. He'll understand, I promise."

"I'll try," Sophie told Kat but wasn't actually sure whether she meant it or not.

"That's all I can ask for. The rest is up to you."

"You're really good at all this..." Sophie gestured her hands between them, trying to find the right words, but her mind had turned to mush "...this deep talking stuff."

"It's what I do, what I went to school for, to get people to open up and give me answers they don't want to. Sometimes, I have to do all the talking, but if I can see a person's mind opening like a door, then I know it is working."

"And did my mind open like a door?"

"It was already open; you just needed to walk through."

"I don't know if I can do that."

"I'll help."

"Thanks, Kat. Thanks for being there for me."

"Always, Sophie."

CHAPTER FIFTEEN

Sophie had promised Kat that she'd try to figure things out with Benny, but what exactly that entailed, she didn't know. So far, it had been a few days, and she was stuck. She didn't even know how to get into touch with him. Should she call? Should she text him? Show up at his door waving a white flag? And then what? They'd talk and everything would magically be okay? It wasn't as simple as Kat had tried to make it seem.

Sophie bordered on the verge of just giving up and going back to her routine, plastering on a smile and forgetting about everything but the present. Faking it until making it. But that was what she had been doing all those years, and although it seemed to work quite well on the surface, the minute her perfectly constructed façade had a rock thrown at it, it shattered. It didn't just crack a little before it slowly spread through the building and came crumbling down. No, her internal wall came down faster than the Berlin Wall, and it destroyed her, as was proof by her state during the previous month.

The knock at her door surprised her. Kat had found Sophie's spare key the first time she had come over and had stopped bothering to knock. She hadn't spoken to any of her friends in a while, and when she did, she pretended to be fine, so none of them would know what was going on with her. Her parents had moved during Kat's medical school because of her father's work. They were pretty close, but only saw each other for the holidays.

"What the..." she trailed off as she looked through the peephole. The last person she expected to see was standing outside her door. It's like the universe had heard her struggles and decided to throw her for a loop just because it could. *Stupid universe.*

She opened the door cautiously. "Benny, what are you doing here?"

"I know that I'm the last person you want to see, and I fully expect you to say no right now, but I need you to come with me."

"I...what? No." They had plenty of things to talk about, but she wasn't going anywhere with him until they talked.

"Please Sophie, it's important."

"Where are we going? And why didn't you call to warn me that you were coming?" She was in defense mode.

"I didn't call because I didn't want to give you time to leave. I'm not above admitting that I was hoping to catch you off guard, which I fully expected would have you coming with me easily." She saw a ghost of a smile on Benny's face and then it was gone. He was really beautiful when he did smile. She hadn't seen enough of that lately. Come to think of it, she hadn't seen a lot of that when they were growing up, either, but when he did smile, it lit up the entire room. Even head over heels for Ethan, when Benny smiled, she looked, and drooled, and then looked some more.

"Don't you think that we should at least talk things through first before we go anywhere?"

"We can, and we will talk when we get there. I know that I have no right to ask, and you have no reason to, but I'm asking you to trust me Sophie." She hesitated and he continued. "You've known me through the good and the bad, you've known me since we were kids; I've made a lot of mistakes in my life, some worse than others, but deep down, you know that I'm the guy you used to be able to talk to, and that, Sophie, took trust. Please, if for nothing else but for the sake of those two kids that we were, please trust me again." He held out his hand to her. She studied his face, really studied it. The shadows under his eyes were so prominent that it looked like he had two black eyes, his cheeks were hallowing out, and as massive as his body still was, she could see that he had lost weight. He had suffered the past month. Kat had said it, but it took seeing him to truly believe it. Kat had been right. He was just as affected by Ethan's loss, by her child's loss as she was.

She put her hand in his, and just like that, she stepped through that door. Whether she kept walking or turned back around was yet to be seen.

*****

After leading her to his car, they drove in silence. It wasn't awkward, but it was far from comfortable. So many times, Sophie opened her mouth to say something, ask where they were going, but just as quickly, she'd close her mouth, the words not forming on her lips. She recognized the direction they were going but refused to believe Benny would take her there. It was only when they drove through the cemetery gates that she was forced to face the facts.

"What are we doing here?" She spoke as she started to unbuckle her seatbelt, the panic in her voice apparent

"Sophie, please, I asked you to trust me, and you did. So please…" he trailed off as he looked at her. The way his eyes pleaded with her had her reluctantly nodding.

"I don't know why you think visiting Ethan's grave is going to help, or how talking here is the best thing."

"You'll see." She could only nod again. He got out of the car and she followed close behind until they made it to Ethan's grave. She gasped, covered her mouth, and then bowed over because wracking sobs had overtaken her.

Ethan's tombstone stood as it always had:

Ethan Michael Negrete
An Angel Taken Too Soon
Beloved Son and Brother

Every time Sophie visited Ethan, every time she looked at that, she broke. It was a natural reaction to miss him, to mourn for him at his gravesite, but it also hurt that it hadn't said he was a beloved father as well.

What had her bawling uncontrollably now was the new stone right beside Ethan's.

Baby Negrete
Your Father's Wings Surround You
As You Ascend to an Angel's Throne

It took her a while to realize that strong arms had wrapped themselves around her waist to keep her from falling to her knees.

"What...what did you do?" Sophie asked through her wet lashes, looking up at Benny as she calmed just enough to speak.

"Closure, Sophie. For both of us, but mainly for you."

"I...I don't understand," she said as she pressed a hand to the new tombstone, Benny's arms still circling her. His eyes were red and splotchy and his cheeks were wet from silent tears, and yet, he held her up, was the support that she needed even if it was obvious he needed comfort, too. She felt safe; she knew he wouldn't let her fall. And God help her, but she didn't feel guilty, even as she stood by Ethan's final resting place.

"You had to say goodbye to Ethan, only to get a glimmer of hope that he still lived, but that was shattered when you lost the baby. You lost Ethan all over again, but you never got to say goodbye a second time. This is for you," he spoke softly.

"And what about you?" Sophie asked genuinely.

"Living each day, Sophie, I figured that was my punishment for Ethan's death. Sometimes living is worse than dying. But when you told me about the baby, I truly didn't understand why I was still alive. It should have been me," he choked. "It should have been me," he repeated as he paused to catch his breath. Sophie didn't dare move. "The guilt weighs me down. I figured that was just more punishment, and yet it wasn't enough because now you had suffered, too. You have to understand, Sophie, that when I lost Ethan, I lost myself. But when I found out that I lost the chance to be an uncle, too, there was nothing left of me to lose. I just wallowed, a shell of myself. I tried to drown my sorrows at the bottom of a bottle, but it was Mason who pointed out that I still had purpose; I still had reasons to live. I love Ethan more than my life, and God knows that I'd have given my life for his ten times over. I *am* to blame for his death, but I can't do anything about that. But I can be there for the rest of my family. And I have family, Sophie – Mason, Kat, their kids, even John, Chain, and Marco are my family. And you, too," he added tentatively. "Mason wisely informed me that sometimes family isn't blood, they're chosen. So this is me saying goodbye to the asshole I was back then, the selfish bastard who didn't care about anyone but himself, and the person who caused his brother's death and so much more. This is goodbye to my guilt so that I can be there for the people who need me now. And you, Sophie, are one of them. Push me, pull me, yell at me, hit me, curse at me, tell me to go away – whatever you want, but I'm here for you. I'm here to tell you that I care about Ethan, I care about the niece or nephew I never got to meet…I care about you."

He hadn't bothered to wipe the tears trailing down his cheeks. He didn't hide his pain from Sophie. He just held her, letting her lean on him the way that she wished he would have back then. Strong even in the face of anguish, soothing when he needed consoling himself. This was the Benny she had known so long ago – this was the Benny who she wished Ethan could look up to, this was the Benny her heart broke for, and this was the Benny her soul cried for.

She turned in his arms and lifted her own to embrace him. His body went rigid for a moment before he buried his head in her hair and she felt him tremble as he cried. Just like that, she physically felt her anger dissipate. Years of suppressed rage, pent-up anger, even an abundance of sorrow was washed away with minutes of tenderness. The heart was a funny thing; it wiped out years of bad with a moment of good, it fought the mind to overpower logic, and if it wanted something bad enough, it omitted reason instantly, and Sophie's heart…it wanted to love.

"Thank you," she whispered. *Thank you for showing me your true self, thank you for opening up to me, thank you for being here for me now – it was never too late, thank you for holding me up when I thought I might fall, and thank you for showing me you care.* They had things to talk about, but for now, this was enough.

CHAPTER SIXTEEN

Benny and Sophie spent another half an hour at the cemetery. They took that time to speak silently with Ethan, Sophie's lost child, and even themselves. They stood side by side, somewhat leaning against each other, but neither spoke aloud. Sophie wasn't sure what Benny had on his mind, but she took the time to tell Ethan everything she felt, even some of the things she only admitted to herself but never spoke to him about, and then she forgave him. She told him that she resented feeling like she was Ethan's second choice, but realized with time that it was never about that. She told him that she was angry that he left her, especially since she felt it was somewhat his fault, but she got that it wasn't by choice. She told him that had she not lost the baby, she would have loved it with all her heart and told him or her all about how wonderful their father was. She finally told him that she didn't blame him. And she told herself that there would always be a place that was meant for Ethan, but it wouldn't hold her back anymore. She hadn't been in a serious relationship thus far for a reason, and that reason was Ethan. She couldn't keep living in the past any longer. She'd never forget him, forget what could have been, but she couldn't live with the "what ifs" any longer. She deserved to get on with her life, and although she knew it wouldn't be easy, she'd finally be able to do that.

She took a moment to whisper words of love to a baby that never was and asked Ethan to take care of their child. She wasn't sure if she believed in an afterlife, or whether Ethan could see her or hear her, but it gave her comfort to think he could, at least in this spot.

She wiped the wetness of her cheeks, pressed a kiss to her lips, and then pressed it to the baby's stone, repeating the same with Ethan. She turned to see Benny watching her, his eyes full of sorrow, tenderness, regret, even longing. What for, Sophie wasn't sure, but there was also hope. And for the first time, she knew that she felt it, too. Hope for letting go, hope for moving on.

This time, she held out her hand to him. "I think we've said enough here."

Benny nodded and put his hand in hers. Sophie couldn't help how it made her feel. His hand enveloped hers, holding tight, his fingers linking with hers, the heat from his palm searing her. It was protective. That was Benny. He had always been reckless with his own life, but he'd never put those he loved in any purposeful danger. How she could have ever blamed him for Ethan, knowing Benny would die before he'd let those he loved be harmed was beyond her. Grief did stranger things to the mind than love did to the heart.

Benny drove Sophie home, and then followed her inside in silent understanding. They sat down on opposite couches but neither said a word. Sophie knew she had to say something. Benny had shared a lot at the cemetery. He had even shared more with his actions, and Sophie had stayed relatively quiet. She just didn't know how to get the million thoughts in her head to form coherent sentences. Her job required her to work with various people on a daily basis. She gave good news, bad news, and all sorts of information with ease, but she couldn't say one word with Benny in front of her. She had never been tongue-tied around him. Even when she looked up to him, an older otherworldly figure, she could speak with him for hours. But not now.

"Sophie, I'm so sorry," Benny started, and it was just what she needed for her mouth to start working.

"No, Benny, *I'm* sorry. It's just…I don't know where to begin," she mumbled to herself. Benny nodded as if he understood. She bet he did. "Ethan was my world, and I watched him struggle to be like you. He was pulling away from me, and neither of us realized it. I resented him…no, I resented *you* for that." She took a breath and closed her eyes to keep from crying any more. She had had enough. "And then he was suddenly gone, and with that, my world was gone, too. I was shattered. I was falling apart, and I didn't know how to keep from drowning. I needed someone to help keep me afloat. I hadn't known that at the time, and I didn't realize until recently that I needed you to comfort me. You see, Benny, I looked up to you, too. If you could stay strong, I was hoping a little bit of that strength would rub off on me, too. I know you were mourning, too, and it was selfish of me to expect you to put your grief aside for mine, but like I said, I didn't even realize that I needed you then. Instead, my resentment turned to hate. It didn't help that I thought you had pushed Ethan to join you in your extracurricular activities." She hated saying "gang." "But it wasn't just that. I hated you for so many reasons that were out of your control. I hated you because Ethan wanted to be like you, I hated you because he wanted your approval, I hated you because you weren't there for me, I hated you simply because I couldn't hate Ethan. You became the source of all that anger, and it helped keep me grounded for a while, especially after I lost my baby, my last shred of Ethan. All the pain I felt, I projected it onto you, and it made my life a little easier. You didn't deserve that. All of Ethan's actions were his own. I'd like to say that I came to that conclusion a long time ago, but Kat helped knock some sense into me. I'm sorry, Benny. I really am."

"You had every right to blame me," Benny told her. "Even before Ethan could walk, his eyes would follow my every movement. Everything I did, he'd do it right behind. He was like my parrot, and when we were younger, I thought it was the best thing. Do you know how great it feels to know that no matter what, there is at least one person in this world who thinks you can do no wrong? That's what I had, but I started taking it for granted. I wanted to do other things with my life, experience things that I had no business being a part of. I should have known Ethan would want to, too, but I just...I just didn't care enough to stop and think. I've blamed myself every day since his death, and I'll continue to blame myself until the day that I die, but I'm still here, and I have to live my life like I'm alive."

"You were a kid yourself, Benny. You shouldn't have had that much responsibility to have to worry about Ethan." Sophie mirrored the words Kat had told her previously.

"Kid or not, he was mine to protect, and I failed him." Sophie knew that she could argue for days, but she'd get nowhere, so she moved closer and put her hand on Benny's, just to tell him it was okay. They stayed that way for a few minutes until Sophie had to ask the question she was dying to know. "I just don't understand one thing. Why did you stick with gangs and crime and violence? Wouldn't his death have forced you to finally see that wasn't the right path for you?"

"It had never been something long-term, and I certainly didn't plan to be a part of it for much longer, but I needed to avenge Ethan's death. And with that came violence."

"How did you..." she trailed off, suddenly understanding just what Benny meant. She should have been appalled, but she was actually grateful that Benny cared enough to shed blood for Ethan. She squeezed his hand to let him know.

"I could have gotten out after that. I didn't really care what happened to me, but I had gotten my friends involved, and they couldn't walk around with a giant target on their backs, so we kept on going with that life. I tried to leave so many times...but when it's the only thing you know, it's hard to start something new. It took a while, but I managed to start new life, Sophie," he added, almost as if he needed her to see that he wasn't still some street thug.

"I get it, Benny, and that's exactly why you're a good person. You put the people you love first. I know you would have put Ethan first, too, even my baby, had you thought things through. You can't be faulted for that."

He pulled his hand from Sophie's and lifted his shirt, exposing his tattooed chest. He pointed directly at his heart, at the tattoo memorial for

Ethan. "See this, Sophie. This is the missing piece that Ethan took with him when he died." She had seen it before, but she still shivered with the impact it had on her and the emotion flowing from Benny's voice. "I'm never getting it back, and that's because I didn't put him first. I look at this every day to remind me never to make the same mistakes I did back then. I don't...I don't know if I'm strong enough without that reminder." He hung his head as if in shame.

"I'm never going to get through to you, am I?" Sophie asked herself more than Benny. "I see the way you are with your friends, with Benji and Katy, even with me. You didn't have to come here. You didn't have to try to make things right with me. Why did you, Benny? Why? It's because you're a good guy. Because you truly care. I love that you memorialized Ethan on your skin, but you don't need a tattoo to remind you to love because you do that all on your own." He looked at her, his eyes shining with spilled tears, willing her to say something more.

She stood and came close to him, kneeling in front of him, taking both his hands in hers. He had given her all his strength; he had done exactly what she had needed him to do. She was the one who could see reason now – thanks to him. Just a few days before, she was a blubbering mess, wallowing in the past and letting it own her. It took less than a day for all that to change. All because of Benny. Now, it was time to give it back. It was time to help him move on because he had done that with her. It was time to tell him the one thing that she knew he needed to hear, even if he didn't.

"I forgive you," she whispered, her voice hoarse as if it hadn't been just used. It wasn't from lack of conviction, but rather with the force of impact that the words had even on herself. Benny opened his mouth slightly as if in shock. She nodded as if telling him that he heard right and then repeated herself. "I forgive you."

He cocked his head to the side as if trying to register whether she was real or a figment of his imagination. And then he pulled her to him so that she was sitting in his lap and his strong arms were around her, his head buried in her hair, and for the second time that day, he cried in her arms. "Thank you," he whispered over and over into her hair. They stayed that way for minutes before finally breaking apart.

"Friends?" Sophie finally asked.

"Family."

CHAPTER SEVENTEEN

That day had been exactly what Sophie needed to snap out of her funk. It was like someone had flipped the switch and she was back to her normal self. She had spent a good amount of time in front of the mirror after Benny had left just staring at the stranger in front of her. She had looked like someone who had been starved and hadn't seen the sun in days. It had been a fairly accurate portrayal, but she didn't like the person she had become any longer.

"No more feeling sorry for yourself," she told her image. "Time to be the strong woman I know you are." Then she proceeded to shower and have a hearty meal. "I need my butt back," she said out loud as if someone was wondering why she was eating so much.

She went back to work two days later, feeling she needed a day to truly recuperate.

"Look at you!" Kat cried when Sophie met her and the twins for lunch the following day. "Happy looks good on you." She smiled.

"Thanks, Kat. I owe you a lot. You helped snap me out of my funk."

"Oh? Was it me or a handsome tattooed man who we both know and love?"

"Why am I not surprised that you know about that?" Sophie shook her head in mock dismay.

"Because you know me too well? And because you know that I know everything."

"You remind me of that movie *Teen Witch*. You remember it? It came out in the eighties," Sophie told Kat.

"Oh my God! I loved that movie!" Kat cried.

"You remember the part where Madame Serena says, 'Madame Serena knows all...sees all...'? Well, yeah, that's you!" Sophie laughed.

"I knew I liked you for a reason." They laughed and joked about how cheesy the movie was. Then Kat brought them back to Benny. "You didn't deny it."

"What are you talking about?" Sophie asked.

"When I talked about Benny and said a man we both knew and loved, you didn't say no."

"Well, yeah, I knew you were talking about Benny, and I know that you know what he did for us...for me."

"He's a really great guy, Sophie. He takes care of the people he loves, and he loves fiercely. He's there for Mason, for me, and for our children in a flash when we need him. He does so much for so many people. He just doesn't see what I see. He doesn't see all the good in him or all the wonderful things he does. There's always been a shadow following him, clouding his eyes sometimes when he doesn't realize anyone is looking."

"I understand that," Sophie told her.

"I know you do, and that's why I knew that you could lean on each other, but you're strong, and independent, and you've accomplished so much in your life. You've been hurt, but I know you can look at yourself in the mirror and be proud of where you stand."

"That's true," Sophie responded, not one hundred percent sure where the conversation was going.

"Benny can't. He doesn't see all the admirable things that he's done in this life or how many people's lives he's touched and affected in a positive way. I can honestly say that I wouldn't be where I am today without him," she told Sophie.

"I'm sure that he knows all this," Sophie responded.

"Oh, he does, the cocky bastard," Kat chuckled. "But I know that he still sees the past when he looks in the mirror. I hope this truce you two have worked out will help him move beyond that."

"I hope so, too," Sophie told Kat honestly. The more she thought about Benny, the more she saw just how great he really was. Back when Ethan died, Sophie had been his brother's girlfriend, and he might have owed her a little closure then, but he certainly didn't owe her anything now. She was a childhood friend at most, an acquaintance at best, and he had taken the time to give her comfort and open up.

"But, look at me; here I go getting off topic. What I meant was the love part. You didn't deny any feelings there. Do I dare say our young Sophie has some for Benny?"

"I...wha? what?" Sophie sputtered. "Where did that come from?"

"Aw, you're blushing, how cute," Kat spoke before taking a squirming Benji in her arms. "I think Sophie likes your godfather," she cooed at him, and he actually calmed down. *Traitorous child.*

"He's shown me a side of himself that I haven't seen since we were kids. And what you've said is true – he's a good guy. Of course, I care about him. But we're friends, Kat."

"Friends," Kat repeated.

"Yep."

74

"If you say so." Kat smiled mischievously.

Sophie changed the subject and the rest of the conversation was far from Benny, but it had gotten Sophie's mind thinking. Did she like Benny? Yeah, of course, she did – but as a friend, that was all.

*****

That day with Sophie had affected Benny more than he wanted to admit.

"You doing okay?" John asked.

"Yeah, I'm good," he said after he went back to work. They were working on fixing up an old warehouse and turning it into a lounge. John and Chain had done most of the work in the past month as Benny wallowed.

"Have you talked to Sophie again?" John asked. The asshole knew exactly where Benny's head was at.

"Nah, giving her some time."

"For what? I thought you guys kissed and made up? Friends, right? Friends talk, hang out."

"We're not that kind of friends."

"Why the fuck not?" John asked.

"We just aren't. Drop it."

"You like her."

"Of course I like," Benny told John.

"Nah, fucker, you like her. Don't deny it. Why else would you play hero for her?"

"I'm far from a hero, asshole. And she was going to have my niece or nephew. I owed it to her."

"Call it whatever you want, Benny, but your head's been up your ass the last week. I know your mind's been on Sophie. Shit, I can't blame you. A body like hers."

"Don't fucking talk about her like that," Benny practically roared.

"Don't like her, my ass." John smiled.

Just then both their phones dinged, and they both looked down. It was a mass text message from Kat.

BBQ at our place. Saturday, 2pm. Be there!

Benny sent a quick *yes ma'am* before he tried to discretely see who else the text was sent to. His heart hammered in his chest when he saw Sophie was on the group text. If she came, that would be the first time they saw each other after their truce. He didn't know how to act around her. They had made peace, even declared they were family, but was that something two grieving people did in the moment and then went their separate ways?

He saw John's reply that he would be there, and then he saw Sophie's response.

I'm in. What should I bring?

Just your wonderful self, Kat responded. *Typical Kat.* It made Benny smile.

"What's that smile about?" John asked.

"Just thinking about how great it's going to feel to kick your ass at soccer," Benny lied. They often played games on Mason's gaming system, soccer being their favorite. The guys were really competitive, but it was all in good fun.

John snorted. "Yeah, buddy, in your dreams."

*****

Saturday couldn't come fast enough. Benny had put all his effort into work, not leaving any room to think about the possible awkwardness between him and Sophie. He wanted it over with. No, he didn't. He couldn't make up his mind.

He arrived late, as usual, and Sophie was already there. Was he supposed to go over and say hi to her? Damn, he was acting like a teenage boy with his first crush.

Just to prove his subconscious wrong, he was going to say hi to her, right after he said hi to Mason and Kat.

"Did you see Sophie?" Kat asked, the little devil. "She looks great, right?"

"Kitty Kat," he said her name as if in warning.

"What?" she asked innocently as she batted her lashes.

"I know what you're trying to do."

"Well, at least that makes one of us because I have no clue what you're talking about," she smiled sweetly. "But Benny, you can't be mean. Go say hi to her."

"You." He pointed at her, but couldn't help the chuckle that escaped his mouth. "You're trouble, Kitty Kat."

"You know it," she said and spun him around and gave him a shove.

"Hey, Sophie," he said as he approached her.

"Benny." The way she said his name as if she was breathless had his thoughts racing in a million directions that weren't suited for public. He could imagine her whispering his name in his ear as he buried himself deep inside, feeling every inch of her glorious skin against his. His jeans felt suddenly tight as he looked at her lips. "How are you doing?" Sophie asked, breaking him from his thoughts.

"I'm good, actually. Got back to work. Had a lot of catching up to do. You?"

"Oh, yeah." She smiled, and it broke the tension they were feeling. "But it feels good, you know? Being busy, feeling needed."

"Yeah, I know what you mean."

They grew silent, each not knowing what else to say.

"This is awkward." Sophie laughed.

"But it shouldn't be," Benny stated. "Come grab a drink with me, and let's sit and talk. We're friends, right?" he smiled.

"Yeah," she said but seemed to be thinking. "Yeah, I'd like that," she said with more conviction. They made their way to the kitchen and Benny grabbed two beers from the fridge. He opened them, and they both leaned against the counter.

"I know that you now I knew you when you were a kid. But I don't know much about what happened between now and then. Tell me what I'm missing," Benny almost demanded.

"What do you want to know?"

"Everything."

They spent the next hour telling each other about their lives. She told him about school, her residency, some funny moments with friends. He told her about work and parts about his life.

"And then I see John running out of the house buck naked screaming about a unicorn stealing his clothes."

They were practically rolling on the floor in tears, laughing so hard at the stories he recalled. Most of them involved dares and alcohol.

"I can't believe he did that," Sophie spoke between breaths.

"A dare's a dare." Benny smiled.

The day went by in the blink of an eye.

"This was nice, Benny."

"Yeah, Sophie, it was."

"I'm glad we're friends," she told him, but the tone sounded nervous. Benny couldn't understand what she had to be nervous about.

"Me, too. Let's do this again, yeah?"

"Definitely."

Air cleared, tension removed, smiles in place...Benny and Sophie were officially friends.

CHAPTER EIGHTEEN

"Can you take care of Benny?" Mason popped his head into Sophie's office.

She hadn't seen him in a little over a week since the BBQ, and although things had gone smoothly between them, she didn't expect them to start becoming best friends after that. It just meant that whenever they saw each other, they could hang out comfortably.

"Uh, sure. Why?" she asked.

"Not sure, didn't have time to get the details. I was on the phone with Kat when he walked in and she said she needed some formula or something for Katy ASAP. Gotta run to the store real quick." Mason's words trailed as he already started heading out.

"Sure, she needed something ASAP," Sophie mumbled to herself. She had a sinking suspicion that Kat was trying to get Sophie and Benny to spend more time together. Nevertheless, she went to the exam room to see what had happened.

"Hey, Benny, what'd the neighbor do this time?" she teased. His responding smile made her heart literally flutter. She had never really paid attention to his looks when they were younger. Sure, she noticed that he was attractive, but he was older and not for her. So she focused on Ethan, the guy she knew would be her equal. Now though, it seemed that all she could do was stare at him. He was beautiful in a rugged way, a little rough around the edges, like he knew things beyond his years. There was always a glint in his eyes and a hint of mischief behind his smile. That had always been there, but it seemed to be more pronounced now. It was alluring. Sophie mentally chided herself for observing these things.

"Nah, this time it's John's fault," he told her.

"John? What'd he do?" She'd known John almost as long as Benny. He was a big guy, extremely intimidating even when he was growing up. He was always pretty silent, too, which just made him seem even more threatening, like he was assessing the situation. Maybe he was, but deep down, Sophie knew that he was gentle unless provoked and had a really good heart. *Huh.* No wonder he and Benny were friends.

"We're converting a warehouse into a lounge," Benny told her. "We were onsite talking to the contractor, and John decided he wanted to get some hands-on experience. He was just trying to show off in front of the contractor's assistant," Benny grinned.

"So what happened?"

"He was too busy making sure the girl was watching and didn't notice that the two-by-four he carried was aimed at my head."

Sophie gasped and walked behind Benny. He had a small cut on the side of his head. It wasn't long, but it was pretty deep and blood trailed down and onto his shirt.

"And where is John now?"

"The fucker wouldn't let me drive. Dropped me off and went back to finalize things."

"How are you getting back?" Sophie asked as she started working on Benny's cut.

"I'll get a cab," he answered as if Sophie wasn't sticking a needle in his head. She hadn't bothered to ask if he wanted local anesthesia; she knew he'd decline.

"I don't have any clients until after lunch. I can drop you off if you'd like."

"I don't want to trouble you," Benny responded.

"It's no big deal. I have to go out to grab lunch anyway."

"Only if you let me buy you lunch," Benny told her, and she found herself smiling at that.

"Deal." She finished his stitches, and they headed out to a café nearby.

They ordered, and Benny paid before they found a table near the window.

"What's it like?" Benny asked.

"What's what like?" Sophie scrunched up her nose in confusion.

"Fixing people, helping them…just making a difference."

"I don't-" she started to protest, but Benny cut her off.

"Yeah, Sophie, you do. I've only ever…" he trailed off, but Sophie knew what he was implying. That he'd only ever hurt people.

"I do what I can, Benny. I'm not a miracle worker or even a genius. I studied the human body and memorized conditions and symptoms, and I match them together. I didn't find the diseases. I didn't create the medicines to treat them."

"Don't say that. Don't downplay what you do." But that was exactly what she was doing. Something inside her didn't want Benny to feel so inadequate, and that was her way of showing him that she wasn't any better than him.

"I'm not. It's just that what I do doesn't make me any better than other people. A woman who feeds the homeless or a guy who donates to charities, or even a person who is there for their friends…that's helping others, too. That's fixing people, Benny. And that's something. So, back at you. Don't downplay what you do, either. You're there for the people you love."

"Haven't always been," he muttered, but Sophie heard him.

"Better late than never," she retorted.

"Sometimes late is too late."

"You're right, sometimes it is, but there is nothing we can do about the past. You said it yourself – it's time to live our lives. So, let's live. No more sad talk for today."

"If you say so." Benny cracked a smile.

"I do." And then Sophie changed the topic and they ate the remainder of their lunch while chitchatting. It was easy and nice, and Sophie found herself truly enjoying Benny's company. When she dropped him off, she actually didn't want their time together to end. He had been the first real friend she'd had in a while. All the other people in her life didn't really know her – they didn't know the things she hid – and therefore, they only got to experience Sophie with a plastic smile. But Benny – and well, Kat and Mason and even John, too – knew the real her. She needed and wanted to cherish those friendships.

*****

"Sophie, I really, really hate to ask, but are you free this Friday?" Kat asked Sophie over the phone about a week later.

"Yeah, sure. Why do you ask?"

"Because I really wanted to have a date night with Mason. He's been stressed lately, and I thought some time away for just us would be nice. But I need someone to watch the kids."

"Of course!" Sophie cried. Kat had quickly turned into one of Sophie's best friends. She'd do just about anything for her. Besides, watching the two cuties was a bonus.

Friday rolled around and Sophie headed toward Kat's place. After knocking on the door, she found herself stuttering. "Wha…what are you doing here?" she asked Benny, who was holding Katy in his arms.

"Oh good," Kat came to the door. "You're here."

"Uh, Kat, I thought you needed me to babysit," Sophie told her.

"I do. Two kids, two sitters." Then she ran back, grabbed Mason, and started pulling him out.

"Kat? What's going on?" Mason asked.

"Oh nothing, both Benny and Sophie volunteered to watch the kids. Isn't that awesome? Let's go," she told him as she dragged him out, a sorry expression on his face as he looked between Sophie and Benny.

"Kitty Kat," Benny called after her.

"Love you too, Benny," she called back and then they were gone.

"Looks like Kat struck again," Benny chuckled.

"Looks like it," Sophie giggled. "I don't get why. We're friends, right? Or is there something I don't know?"

"Nope, all good here," Benny answered.

"Well, if you want to head out, I can take care of them."

"Nah, Kat's right, it's easier with two people, unless you have other plans?" He posed it as a question more than a statement.

"Two sitters, it is," Sophie told him.

The night had been all sorts of fun, between Benji peeing on Benny when he changed his diaper to Katy crying every time Sophie put her down for over an hour to both kids giggling uncontrollably when Benny sang to them. In their defense, Benny was not a singer. Sophie had to stop herself from laughing several times. It was hours before the kids went to sleep, and both Benny and Sophie plopped down on the couch exhausted.

"How do you do this by yourself?" Sophie asked, knowing Benny had babysat several times on his own.

"It's a struggle, but I love them."

"Yeah, they're great, but I'm glad they're finally asleep."

"Me, too."

They found a movie to watch on TV, but the next thing Sophie knew, Kat was waking them up gently. Sophie opened her eyes to realize her head was on Benny's shoulder and his arm was around her, holding her and keeping her safe. For a brief moment, she actually resented Kat for waking her up. She hadn't slept that well in ages, and she felt so warm and not alone. It was a wonderful feeling.

When she said goodnight to Benny after they walked out together, she blamed just waking up and her head feeling a bit fuzzy for the words that came out of her mouth. "I like hanging out with you. We should do it more often."

Benny seemed to ponder her statement, his mouth slightly ajar, his brows furrowed before he responded with a dazzling smile. "Yeah, we should. I'll call you this week, and we'll grab dinner."

And he did. He called her two days later, and they went out *as friends* the next day. That was the start of their friendship. They hung out several times a week, sometimes going to dinner, sometimes watching movies together, sometimes getting drinks, but it was always nice, and Sophie had fun getting to know Benny. It was like being with the little boy who sat and talked with her for hours when she was a kid…but better.

CHAPTER NINETEEN

Spending time with Sophie had become Benny's favorite pastime. He loved the way that their conversation would flow easily between them, the way she laughed with her head thrown back, how her eyes twinkled when they teased each other, how she'd fall asleep on his arm when they watched TV together…shit, he just loved pretty much anything to do with Sophie.

He knew he had chased away the shadows in her life, but his were still there, just lurking under the surface. But when he was with her, they were pushed deep down into the recesses of his mind. He didn't deserve to feel the way he did around her. He knew no matter which direction life had taken him, and no matter what Mason had told him or what Sophie believed, he wasn't a good guy beneath it all. Ethan was gone, his child with Sophie a distant memory, and here Benny was spending time with Sophie like she was his girl. And damn if he didn't want her to be. She was beautiful – inside and out. He was a selfish bastard, so he couldn't stop being with her, but he'd never make a move on her. Although Ethan was long gone, she was still his girl. He knew realistically that Sophie would find someone and move on, but it wouldn't be with him. Not that she'd want him. He was someone she could relate to, so she spent time with him, but he was still a street thug…reformed or not, he was what he was, and Sophie deserved better.

It didn't stop his feelings from going on a rollercoaster whenever he was around Sophie…or even when he thought about her. It sure as hell didn't stop his imagination from thinking about her chocolate eyes staring into his as her long legs wrapped around his body. His mind was extremely creative when it came to Sophie and her body. He saw her in lingerie, in skintight dresses, in bikinis only women in Brazil could get away with, and of course, he pictured her naked too many times to count. And his dreams…damn, he'd woken up hard more times lately than he did when he was a teenage boy. He was surprised that he wasn't walking around with a bulge in his pants more often.

It didn't help that he couldn't seem to stop himself from flirting with her, and she liked to give it right back.

A couple months after they first started hanging out, Sophie had been at Kat and Mason's helping Kat go through the kids' things. He wasn't sure why Kat needed help doing that, but Kat simply gave him a look, then rolled her eyes and said, "Men."

Later, Sophie had told him that Kat had asked Sophie to be the voice of reason when it came to determining what to trash and what to save. Kat had a hard time letting things go even if Benji and Katy had outgrown them. She'd whine and say things like, "But Benji wore this the first time he made the pucker face." He didn't even know what a pucker face was or how Kat remembered that, but supposedly, Sophie took charge when Kat started crying about tossing things out.

Mason had told the guys to come over and watch the game while the girls did their thing. Benny was pretty sure that Mason needed a buffer between an emotional Kat, a slightly controlling Sophie, and two infants who were beginning to become a handful.

Benny had been the first guy to arrive. "Honey, I'm home," he called out as he walked through the door. He was no more than a few steps in when he watched Sophie walk out of the kids' room, trip on a toy on the floor, and pretty much sprawl at Benny's feet.

"Falling at my feet." Benny smiled. "Now that's a greeting," he chuckled.

"Oh, shut up, you," Sophie tried to scold, but the smile gave her away as he helped her up.

"You know, Sophie, if you want to kiss the ground I walk on, there are better ways to do it," he teased.

"And there are better things to kiss," she responded.

Benny turned so his butt was pointing at her. "If you want to kiss my ass, you only had to ask." To which, she slapped his butt and then laughed.

"Now, children, children…we already have two in the house, well, three if you count Mase. We don't need anymore," Kat said as she walked out.

"You love this big kid," Mason said as he came around the corner.

"Yeah, I do," she responded and then kissed him softly on the lips. Benny looked at Sophie at this moment, and he caught the longing look on her face. It was only there for a brief moment, but it was there. He hated that she felt that way, that she didn't have that someone special in her life, and he knew deep down that he had prevented her from having that with Ethan, but he wasn't going to dwell on it. And yet, when he thought of her with someone – even with Ethan, had he still been alive – he was jealous, which was ridiculous, but he felt it nevertheless.

Either way, when they bantered like that, his stupid heart reacted in a way that it shouldn't.

About a month after that, they were at Sophie's place. She had bought some new paintings, a couple decorative pictures, and some random décor pieces to put around her place. She hadn't lived there long, but was in the mood to make it cozier. She had asked Benny if he wouldn't mind helping her. Of course, he didn't.

"Move it to the right...no, back to the left. Hmm...I don't know."

"Will you just pick a spot already?" Benny huffed. They had spent almost three hours doing things like that. "You are the most indecisive person I've ever met," he complained.

"I just want it perfect," she insisted. "This is my home, and I want it to feel...homey."

He couldn't say no to her when she said things like that. Heck, he couldn't say no to her regardless. If she knew the thoughts he had or the power she had over him, she'd probably throw him out. Or maybe she'd use him even more. No, she wasn't like that. She'd probably let him down gently, not that he needed to be let down. He knew that she was way out of his league, but even if he hadn't been, he'd never try anything with her anyway.

"Sophie, please, for the love of God, tell me where you want this," he urged her.

"Oh, you big baby, here let me show you." He set it down and started to trade spots with her. As she tried to move around him, she knocked over the vase that was on the coffee table.

He dove for it, trying his best to save it, but apparently Sophie had the same idea.

"Ouch," she laughed as they bumped heads. Somehow, the vase fell unharmed, although the fluffy rug probably helped cushion the fall. "I knew you were thickheaded, but damn, Benny, that's real thickheaded," she laughed.

"And your skull is oh so soft," he chuckled as he rubbed his head. He lifted his head to the realization that their faces were mere inches away. He only had to lean in a bit and he could taste her lips once more, feel the softness and the warmth against his mouth, play his tongue against hers. He stopped laughing, his eyes focused on her parted lips. He knew his breath had become shallow, and he could have sworn hers did, too. He wanted to move closer, he wanted to dive in. His heart contemplated, but then his mind stepped in. *You can't*, it told him. *You can't do this. She's not yours.*

He cleared his throat and physically shook his head to stop his racing heart. The spell was broken. They stood up and he took a moment to compose himself. Sophie grabbed the picture and they continued to bicker about placement the rest of the day. But it was moments like this that had Benny's heart contending with his mind, his *logical* mind that is. Luckily, logic always won out.

CHAPTER TWENTY

The only time Sophie and Benny kissed, it was but a whisper. For an instant, though, Sophie relished in the feelings it invoked. And then it was followed by sorrow. That had all changed now. The despair she felt was gone and she was starting to feel truly alive for the first time. She hadn't even realized that she was only half living before she was able to let go of her sadness, let go of her past. And now, she found herself spending more and more time with Benny. He was an excellent companion and an even better friend. The problem was that she wanted to kiss him. She wanted to feel his lips brush hers, his mouth tantalize hers, his tongue tease hers. She wanted him in ways that she shouldn't, but she did.

No matter how far they'd come, how far *she'd* come, and no matter how grounded Benny seemed, he was still the same Benny – full of big aspirations and pins under his butt. She couldn't give into her feelings because she knew Benny wasn't the staying kind, and she would miss him and his friendship too much if they complicated things with her emotions. She'd never be enough for him, not that he wanted her. Benny was a go-getter, and if he had wanted Sophie, he would have had her by then, not that she would have tried all that hard to stop him. But he hadn't. She saw that as proof that her feelings were all one-sided.

It didn't help when Kat would make comments about how wonderful Benny was. Sophie knew that. She had learned it firsthand as they grew closer the past few months. Then Kat would mention how nice Benny looked, but once again, Sophie knew that, too. She had been staring at his gorgeous face and his hard body every time they hung out. She was pretty sure Benny caught her ogling him a couple times, but she managed to always play it off. And of course, Kat would comment about how Sophie and Benny made such a cute couple. Now, that was just cruel. Sophie hadn't had any type of relationship in years; she hadn't wanted one. However, for the first time in what seemed like forever, she was ready, but she just couldn't find the desire to get out there and start dating. She wanted to spend time with Benny instead. For all intents and purposes, they did act like a couple, but they certainly weren't. And that would never happen.

Sophie was over at Kat's place a few weeks later just hanging out, playing with the kids, and chatting about everything and anything. Mason had been trying to fix his gaming system for the past hour, and they had been laughing at the cursing and whining that had been coming from the living room. They had decided to stay hidden in the children's room because they didn't want to "get hit by any flying objects unintentionally," Kat had said as she laughed. "Mason thinks he's a handyman, but he's not good at the technical stuff. He usually gets Benny or John to help him."

A few minutes later, they heard John come in.

"See," Kat smirked. They headed out to say hello and then stayed in the dining room to continue their gossip. Meanwhile, John fixed the system in under five minutes and the boys started playing some game. When Kat heard one of the kids cry, she got up to go check on them, and then Sophie heard a second wailing. She got up to go help Kat, but Mason stood, "I got it."

"You sure?"

"Yeah, I'm sure. John's tired of me kicking his ass." He smiled.

"You wish," John chuckled.

Mason left the room and John came over to Sophie. "How have things been?" John asked.

"Wow, John, I think that's the most you've said to me...ever," Sophie teased.

"You've been a bit preoccupied," he said as he raised his eyebrows. "Things with Benny going good?"

"Yeah, he's a great friend," Sophie responded.

"Friend, huh?"

"Not you, too!" Sophie cried.

"Hey, hey," John put his hands up in mock surrender, "I'm just saying that you guys are awfully cozy for friends."

"That's because he's really an amazing person. He's there for me when I need him. He helps with anything I ask him to. He's just...he's really great."

"Yeah, he is good about that." John nodded. "Once you're in his circle, you're in for life. I knew when he paid your hospital bills that he'd always watch over you."

"What?" Sophie gasped. She couldn't believe what she was hearing. "What are you talking about?"

"Don't worry, Sophie, I know about it. I had been checking on you for Benny. After Ethan had died, when you were grief-stricken and hospitalized, Benny paid your bill. It took a lot of convincing to get him to let go of the past after that." Sophie had only been half listening, the words John was saying slowly processing. She remembered her hospital stay. She hadn't been "sick with grief." She had miscarried. Her parents had been disappointed in her when they found out she was pregnant, but she only knew that because she heard her dad tell her mom that. They never said a bad word to her. They visited her in the hospital rather than stay with her, and her mom patted her on the back and said everything would be okay. It was their way of saying they cared. And she knew they did, they were just…that was just how they were.

She hadn't thought twice about the bills, although she should have known that even insurance wouldn't cover all the costs she had accrued. If she had to think about it, she always assumed her parents had paid the remainder of the bills. They never talked about it, but she should have known they didn't have that kind of money. And now, to learn Benny had watched after her? Made sure she was taken care of? Even paid for her hospital bills? She wondered briefly what would have happened had he learned the real reason for her hospital stay back then before she pushed those thoughts out of her mind. She wasn't dwelling on the past any longer.

"John…I don't understand." She comprehended what he had said, even started processing it, but it wasn't making sense just yet.

"You didn't know?" he asked surprised. "I'm sorry, Sophie. I just assumed that Benny had told you. He was in a bad place himself then, but he asked me to check on you. I did, but when you were hospitalized, it was too much for Benny, so he let you go, but not before he made sure that whatever your insurance didn't cover was paid. I shouldn't have said anything; it wasn't my story to tell. I just…I thought you knew."

"Why?" Sophie asked. "Why did he do it?"

John looked at her like she'd asked a redundant question. Maybe she had, but she needed to hear the words. "Because he wanted to make sure you were okay. Because he cared about you, Sophie. He always has…more than he's ever admitted, even to himself. That never stopped."

It was too much. It was overwhelming. Benny *had* been there for her when she needed him. In his own way, but still, he'd been there. She had already forgiven him for his role in everything, she'd realized her wish that he'd been there for her after Ethan's death was childish, and God help her, she had feelings for him that were more than friendly. And now, to find out that he hadn't let her go through it all on her own…it was just too much.

"I…I have to go," she stuttered.

"No, wait, Sophie, sit, calm down."

"John…I have to go…I have to…Benny." She couldn't form complete sentences. "Please tell Kat that I had to go and I'll call her later," she called out as she turned to John.

"I'm sorry," he responded, but he had a Cheshire cat smile on his face, and somehow she didn't think he was truly sorry.

*****

Sophie pounded on Benny's door, not sure what she was going to say. She had thought about the ramifications of this new information during the entire drive over. Would she thank him? Would she ask him to explain himself? Would she inquire as to why he stopped keeping tabs on her after she was out of the hospital? Would she yell at him for not telling her sooner so she could have saved them both the trouble of thinking he was an uncaring asshole back in the day?

She continued to pound the door for another minute or so.

"I'm coming, I'm coming." She heard Benny's voice on the other side, but her fists didn't take stock of the situation. They just kept banging on his door.

It swung open and Sophie's hand stopped mid-knock. She froze at the sight before her. She had clearly interrupted his shower because Benny stood before her with only a towel draped low on his hips, water droplets peppering his skin, his hair wet and tousled, a day-old scruff showing on his strong jaw, all his tattoos on prominent display for her watering mouth. She was surprised she hadn't swallowed any flies with how wide her jaw had probably dropped.

"Sophie?" he asked, and by the tone in his voice, she was sure that hadn't been the first time he said her name. She had lost all train of thought. "Is everything okay?" The worried expression on his face didn't go unnoticed, and she dropped her hand quickly, realizing it was still up in the air.

"I...uh...yeah, everything's fine. It's just...I know what you did."

"What I did?" Benny asked.

"I know you watched over me after Ethan died."

"How did you...John," he answered his own question before he could finish asking it. "Are you here to tell me that I should have minded my own business?"

"I'm here to thank you," she whispered, her voice hoarse, her eyes having a hard time staying focused on his. He stepped to the side to let her walk in, but when she moved to step inside, her body brushed his. She stopped, her body ever so slightly touching. Even with all her clothes on and the cool air, the dampness of his skin, she could feel the heat of his body caressing hers. Her breath hitched as she looked up into Benny's eyes. His were smoldering, his eyes glued to the shallow rise and fall of her chest.

"Thank you, Benny," she whispered, and Benny's eyes trailed to her lips. "Thank you for being there for me. For watching out for me. For being you. It means so much to me...*you* mean so much to me. I just..." And then her lips were on his. She wasn't even sure if she had moved toward him or he had pulled her toward him. Although, she was pretty sure that she had leaned in for the kiss, but she felt tingles throughout her entire body as his tongue plundered her mouth.

He kicked the door closed, their mouths still glued together, and brought his hands to her face, cupping her with his palms. She moaned into his mouth and brought her hands to rest on his hips. His naked hips. His *very* naked hips. She broke away and looked down. His towel was no longer around his hips but pooling at his feet. And he was clearly enjoying the taste of her, his hardness pointing directly at her as if saying, "yep, you."

She trailed a finger down the "V" and he sucked in a sharp breath before he grabbed her hands with his.

"Sophie, no. God, I'm sorry. I keep fucking things up with you." He bent down to pick up the towel, but she put a hand on him to stop him.

"Don't," she said softly.

"I'm sorry, I shouldn't have done that," he told her.

"Benny, I want you."

"You don't know what you're saying."

"Benny, look at me. Hear what I'm telling you. I want you." She made sure to punctuate each word. He growled deep in his throat before he captured her mouth once more. He picked her up, his lips not leaving hers as he moved them to the bed.

He put her down gently and stood there, his eyes scanning her still clothed body while she racked in the full package that was Benny. "I want you, Benny," she repeated as she started unbuttoning her blouse. He watched, enraptured as she removed every item of clothing, slowly, torturously.

"Beautiful," he told her when she was laying on the bed, naked, displayed for him. "You're too beautiful for words." She felt his words and the awe in his tone through her entire being. "God, Soph." That was the first time he had ever used that nickname on her, and she suddenly loved it. It sounded so reverent coming from his mouth, the way he said it, like she was the ultimate prize. "I've dreamed of this so many times. I've pictured you right here, just like this, more times than I can remember. And never was it as good as reality. Are you sure?" he asked, the expectation that she'd turn him down apparent in his tone.

If Sophie hadn't been sure of what she was about to do before, she was definitely sure now. His words made her tremble, the way he stared at her made her moan, and when she whispered, "I'm sure," and he covered her body with his, she felt more alive than she ever had.

He held himself propped up on his hands around her head as his lips teased hers. It was his way of promising to be gentle with her, take care of her, cherish her. She loved that, but she didn't want gentle. She wanted Benny. She brought her hands behind his head and pushed down so that the force of their kiss bruised both their lips. She arched her hips up and was rewarded with Benny's hips grinding down as he groaned.

"You're making it hard to go slow," he whispered against her lips.

"I don't think you're having any issues in the *hard* department," she teased and drew his lower lip into her mouth as he chuckled lightly.

"Fuck, Soph," he moaned as she raked her nails down his back. "I've been dying being around you and not doing a damn thing. So unless you want this over before it starts, you'll let me be in control." Before she could respond, he grabbed both her hands from behind him and pinned them above her head. He kissed her fiercely on the lips to stop any retorts she had in mind. He ground his hips into her again and that more than shut her up.

She felt more than saw the triumphant smile on his lips as he peppered kisses along her jaw until he settled in the crook of her neck. He kissed a trail down her neck, between her breasts, stopping to suck on each nipple. She arched her back as his tongue swirled around each peak. "More," she whispered as his hand made its way to her core.

"Gladly," he whispered against her skin as his lips continued their downward descent. She felt his lips just brush against her before she felt his nip at her thighs.

"Benny." She spoke his name as a plea, but a plea for what, she wasn't sure.

"Look at me," he commanded, and she obeyed. She watched as his mouth devoured her and his fingers plied her open, his eyes locked on hers the entire time, a glint in his eyes that was a mix of awe and hunger. It was only moments before she cried out for the first time.

As she rode out her wave of ecstasy, she was vaguely aware of the sound of a wrapper ripping. *Condom*, she thought somewhere in the deep recesses of her mind.

"Sophie," Benny whispered her name as he held himself poised at her entrance. It was a request, an assurance, an appeal to continue.

"Please," she whispered. She wanted him. No, she needed him.

Before she could finish her own thought, she felt him fill her and then he stilled.

"So fucking good," he said. "So fucking good," he repeated.

"Benny, please," she responded. It was her way of asking him to move, to finish what they had started, and he obliged.

As he moved inside her, he kissed her, stroking her tongue with his own, mimicking the rhythm of their bodies. She felt herself start to shutter. She was close.

"Oh God, Benny," she moaned into his mouth as her hands tightened around him. As soon as she found her release, Benny groaned and shuttered with his climax. Just like that, she could no longer comprehend the world as anything but stars, fireworks, and explosions...and Benny.

Definitely Benny. Sophie was no stranger to intimacy, but nothing had ever felt like that. It wasn't the sex, although Benny definitely could win an award for his part. It was the way his body melted into hers; it was the way her soul called to his. If there was an afterlife, she hoped it felt exactly like that moment had.

"Better than any dream." Benny spoke after he collapsed beside her and drew her body into his. "Never tire of that," he said more to himself than to her, but Sophie had heard, and she found herself smiling as she snuggled in close to him.

"Me neither," she said quietly before exhaustion took over. But the last thing she remembered was the feel of Benny's arms around her, and she had never felt that safe before in her life. He was her protection, her security; he was her shelter...from herself.

CHAPTER TWENTY-ONE

Benny had been with his fair share of women. More often than not, he had a night of fun and then they'd part their separate ways. Occasionally, he'd have a friend with benefits, but when they'd get too clingy, he'd hightail it out of there as fast as he could. It's not that he didn't want to settle down, especially after seeing Mason get his happily ever after; it's just that no one had ever caught his attention that way. But one night with Sophie, and he was addicted. He knew he wouldn't be able to go back to being friends after that. He had found a rush like he'd never experienced. All those years of chasing bigger and better dreams, and never really finding it…but now he knew what bliss felt like.

Imagine that moment when something truly fantastic happened to you, so great that you actually wanted to pound your fists and scream "yes" as loud as you could. It was like adrenaline pumping through you for just a few seconds, but you are practically high with excitement. That was what being with Sophie was like for Benny – except it didn't just last a moment, it was constant.

He'd been on the verge of feeling that since they had become friends, but he knew, deep down, that once he had a taste of her, he'd be doomed. When he woke up the next day to realize Sophie was still in his arms, he wasn't going to let her go. He watched her sleep, so peaceful, so wonderful, so beautiful. If she regretted it, he'd be gutted, but he'd convince her otherwise. When her eyes fluttered open, and a small smile appeared on her lips, he breathed a sigh of relief.

"You're mine now, Soph," he had simply stated as she turned in his arms to look at him.

"I know," she continued to smile. "But you know what that means?" she asked.

"What?"

"You're mine, too."

"Been yours, Soph…been yours."

Benny had never experienced such joy, such satisfaction in life before as he did dating Sophie. For the next two months, he understood exactly what Mason and Kat felt. He got why Mason would often watch Kat as she flittered across the room or why Kat's face would light up when she talked about Mason, even when they were arguing. Although, that was more of a red-tinged glow, but a glow nonetheless.

He knew that he had a goofy smile on his face most of the time, but he didn't care. He was well and truly happy. Not that he and Sophie were perfect all the time. They had their first argument a week after they started dating about where they were spending the night. Sophie had stayed at his place almost every night that week, mostly because Benny couldn't handle the thought of not being with her, and pretty much guilt-tripped her to stay over. After a week, though, Sophie wanted to spend the night in her bed. Benny had no problem going to her place, but that wasn't the issue. He thought she wanted to spend the night at her place *alone*. It took them a bit of arguing and some complaining before they realized they misunderstood each other.

"Benny, I love waking up in your arms. Of course, I want to spend the night with you," she huffed after they realized what the fight was about. "I just want to be in my own bed."

"Anything you want, Soph," he told her, "as long as I'm with you." He had been dying to tell her that they should just move in together since he didn't plan to spend a night apart for as long as he lived, but he knew it was too much too soon. He went from being a bachelor to a one-woman man in the blink of an eye, and it was all because of Sophie.

"Finally, man," John had told Benny when Benny informed him that Sophie was his girl the day after they first made love. "You guys have been running circles around each other for too long. We were on the verge of placing bets to see how long before you two gave in."

"You're lucky I love you, Johnny," Benny teased.

"Nah, Benny, you're lucky I'm not over there or I'd kick your ass for calling me Johnny," he laughed. "But seriously, I'm happy for you. She's a great girl, and you deserve some good in your life."

"Thanks, John."

"Anytime, bro."

When Sophie had answered Kat's call on his phone later that same morning, he had been on the opposite side of the room and could still hear Kat's squeal through the phone.

"Tell me good news, Sophie," she had said so loud that Benny heard through the phone.

"Good news," Sophie teased. And that was when the shriek heard around the world came into being.

Since then, things had stayed the same but had also drastically changed. They continued to hang out, but this time, there was an ease about their behavior toward each other. They still bantered, they ran errands together, watched movies, and hung out with their friends. Benny even met Sophie's other friends. They met her girlfriends for drinks so she could introduce him. One sneered at his tattoos, another couldn't keep her hands to herself, and the third seemed okay. They were all nice enough, but he understood why Sophie hadn't been too close with them. They weren't the kind of people you could share your secrets with and know they'd have your back. It was no wonder she had grown so close to Kat.

Sophie even got to meet Trent, one of Kat's best friends, whom she had met when she lived in the apartment Mason had rented for her. Trent had met "the one" and moved to be with him, but since then, Trent had met about three more "the ones." He was planning on moving back soon, though, and part of his trip had been scoping out apartments.

"Oh Benny, I like her," Trent had told him when he met Sophie at Kat and Mason's place. "She's spunky. Reminds me of Kat. Oh! The fun I'll have with those two. Yep, definitely moving back."

When Eddie came back from school for the weekend, Kat and Mason had a barbecue, and even Eddie had been drawn to Sophie.

"You know, Sophie, my classes are starting to get difficult, and with the kids, it's getting harder for Mason to help when I need it. Can I get your number so I can ask you questions when I need help?"

"Sure!" Sophie had exclaimed, obviously happy to be included as part of the family.

"Slick, kid, real slick." Benny had laughed, knowing exactly what Eddie was playing at.

"And maybe, you can come visit me at school and give me some in-person training," Eddie added with a wink in Benny's direction.

"Soph, babe, he's playing you," Benny told her as he laughed. "The kid's a genius and he knows it. He just wants in your pants."

Sophie looked at Benny like he had grown two heads, but then she looked at the smirking faces of everyone around her before narrowing her eyes and turning back to Eddie.

He just shrugged, a smirk on his lips, "Hey, it was worth a try."

Everyone burst out laughing. "Eddie Andrew Boyd," Kat tried to discipline, but was too busy giggling, "not cool."

"Love you, too, Kat," he responded, and she smiled wider.

Benny knew he loved Sophie – no, he was *in love* with Sophie before they even started dating; he just never admitted it to himself. He acknowledged that first night, but his feelings just got stronger each passing day. He had opened his mouth to tell her that he loved her on several occasions, but there never seemed to be a right moment. Truth be told, he didn't think Sophie felt the same way and he didn't want to scare her off. He had always had her in the back of his mind, even when he didn't realize it, and when she came back into his life, it took a lot to keep those feelings at bay. Now that they were at the forefront of his mind, it was a constant struggle not to blurt it out. But Sophie had hated him for the better part of her life, and only recently started seeing him in a better light. He wasn't going to do anything to jeopardize what they had.

Nevertheless, things were great. So, when after two months, Sophie started pulling away from Benny, he didn't understand what happened. It started with her telling him she wasn't feeling well and didn't want to get him sick. He came to her place, but she sent him away. This lasted a few days, and when he found out from Mason that she had called in sick, he believed her. But then she started finding other excuses not to see him. Then she claimed she needed to visit her parents last-minute and took a week off. He called her several times a day for that week, but she only texted him once to say that she was okay but was really busy and would call him when she had a chance. She never did.

"I'm losing her, Mase," he told Mason after about a month of avoidance. "If I haven't already lost her."

"I'm sorry, Benny, I really am. I wish I knew what was going on, but even Kat is stumped."

"I love her," Benny admitted out loud for the first time.

"Have you told her?" Mason asked.

"No, I didn't want to scare her off, but look what good that did me," he sighed almost in defeat.

"Then tell her now."

"I've tried to reach her, but she keeps shutting me out. I don't know what to do. I can't lose her. She's given me back something I thought I lost a long time ago. I won't survive it if she leaves me, too."

"You will, Benny, you've got us. We're your family and we love you."

"I know, but it's not the same."

"Then don't give up. Fight for her."

"I've tried."

"This is trying? Nope, Benny, this is wallowing. Don't forget I've seen you in action. You've been my partner in crime, and you did better fighting beside me than you're doing now."

"It's easier being on the sidelines."

"I know, I know, but you're not the guy who sits and allows self-pity to take over. If anything, that's me," Mason tried to joke. "Now do something about it."

"But what?" Benny asked.

"That's on you. I did some drastic things…with your help, so I know you have it in you."

Just like that, a light went off in Benny's head. It was a long shot and risky, but desperate times called for desperate measures. "I know just what to do."

CHAPTER TWENTY-TWO

Sophie was a complete mess. Things had been going great with Benny. No, "great" didn't do it justice. She had felt like she could walk on the moon with no oxygen tank required. Benny was all the air she needed. When he touched her, she felt like every fiber of her being was on fire. When they made love, the way he played her body, she felt like he was a concert cellist and she was his instrument. She'd never felt that way ever.

It tore her to pieces to realize that. It meant that Ethan hadn't gotten to her the way Benny had. She felt so guilty to feel that way, but she couldn't control her emotions any more than the sky could stop being blue. When she showed up at Benny's that night, she hadn't planned on being with him, but with everything she knew about him, everything she felt about him, it was bound to happen. The switch that kept her feelings in check had been flipped, and there was no going back.

When Benny responded to her, she had been both shocked and elated. They had fallen asleep in each other's arms. When she woke, she was afraid things would be awkward, but Benny simply told her she was his, and all her worries ceased to exist.

From that point forward, they were a couple. She hadn't had a real boyfriend since Ethan. Sure, she had dated, even long term, but no one felt like a partner to her. Benny did, though. The more she thought about it, the worse she felt toward Ethan.

She admitted her concerns to Kat, who asked her a series of questions.

"Did Ethan love you?"

"Yes," Sophie answered without hesitation.

"Did he want you to be happy?"

"Absolutely."

"And are you?" Kat asked.

"Very," Sophie admitted shyly.

"Then why do you feel guilty?"

"Because I've moved on...with Ethan's brother."

"Well, Ethan loved Benny, right?"

"Of course."

"Then it actually makes perfect sense. The two people he loved the most together."

"I'm not sure that's how it works," Sophie responded dryly.

"You wanted my professional advice, didn't you?"

"Yes."

"Well, there you have it. You deserve to be happy, so does Benny, and if you make each other happy, then that's what is meant to be. Hey, for all you know, Ethan's looking after you both and bringing you together."

She still felt a bit of nagging guilt every now and then, but Kat's words made her feel better.

Now, though, she was crumbling inside. And it was all her own doing. She should have known she'd fall for Benny. She should have expected it. He was caring, he was thoughtful, and he looked at her like she had created the earth. He made her feel like she could do no wrong, and he treated her with reverence. Dare she say she had never felt more cherished in her life? She hated comparing him to Ethan, but secretly, deep down, she knew things with Ethan had been a fire that was slow burning, constant, always providing warmth on cold days. But with Benny – the fire was an inferno, the flames consuming everything in their wake, the heat scorching her skin, and she was a lover of hot temperatures.

Benny had tried to cook her dinner the previous month. He had actually cooked little things here and there, and he wasn't a bad cook, but he had never made a big dinner for her.

"What's the occasion?" she asked.

"Every day with you is an occasion," he responded and smirked.

"What a charmer," she responded.

"Anything to get in your pants," he said with a wink and a laugh.

"Oh really?" she teased as she started unbuttoning her pants.

The next thing she knew, they were basking in the afterglow on his couch and dinner was burned.

"Going out or ordering in?" Benny chuckled.

"Ordering in," she responded.

"Pizza?" he asked and she nodded.

He stood and got the telephone to order. She stared at his body, the smooth planes, the ripples, the many tattoos. She loved the way his body moved. Sometimes he'd stalk, particularly when he was walking toward her, like a caveman claiming his woman. Other times, he seemed to glide effortlessly. He looked rough but had an easy smile. He turned and winked at her as a smile lit up his face at her obvious perusal of him. She felt it all through her core.

Her eyes locked on the tattoo she knew was a memorial to Ethan. *Forgive me, Ethan*, she thought to herself, *but I love him*. She froze. *Where did that come from?*

She couldn't love Benny. She didn't love him. She hadn't loved anyone since Ethan, and well, we know how that had ended. She hadn't allowed herself to open up to anyone, not just because she had been holding back her pain, but also because she couldn't handle loving someone again.

"Everything okay, Soph?" Benny asked when he came back to the couch.

"Oh, uh, yeah, just getting a headache."

The rest of the night was filled with tension, and she knew Benny noticed it, but she just kept telling him she was coming down with a migraine, or maybe worse. She wanted to leave right then and there, but she knew Benny wouldn't let her go. She spent the night in Benny's arms, but sleep hadn't claimed her. Her mind was working overtime. She tried to reason with herself that she didn't love Benny, that the thought was just a glitch. She told herself that she'd wake up the next day and things would be back to normal, and she could continue being with Benny. But when morning came and she looked at Benny and stupid love filtered into her thoughts, panic set in. She couldn't do this. She couldn't love him and then lose him. She wouldn't be able to take that again.

She hadn't dealt with it well with Ethan, and as much as she had loved him, she knew she loved Benny more. If she really wanted to admit it, she'd probably loved Benny all her life, starting with a little kid looking up to the cool older neighbor. She'd always been infatuated with him. And the hate she felt toward him? She had heard before that the people who can hurt you the most are the ones you love the most because love gives them that power. She hated him because he hurt her – because he wasn't there for her. But it hadn't been his job to be there. It was simply because deep down, she loved him and needed him. It took her all this time to open up her heart and her mind and let the emotion creep out. And once it was out, it wasn't going back in.

She avoided Benny at all costs the past month. She even called in sick to work, and then took an emergency leave of absence, citing her parents needing her. Really, she got a hotel room a few blocks away because she couldn't keep pushing Benny away. She knew she'd cave and then where would that leave her? Broken and alone. She couldn't take that.

She made excuses with Kat, ignored Mason, even disregarded her friends, who would never notice anything was wrong with her. She had spent the better part of that month fighting tears, crumbling to pieces, convincing herself she didn't love Benny, and telling herself she'd be okay. She wasn't. She was far from okay. "Okay" wasn't even a word in her vocabulary. "Distress" was, though. "Misery," too. "Despair" worked also. "Fear," "anxiety," "panic," and "sorrow" were all words she knew very well. She had lived them before, but they were ten times worse now. If she left Benny before he could leave her, then she figured she'd be fine. But it hadn't worked out so well thus far. She was grieving for him before she even lost him.

Her phone rang and Benny's face lit up the screen. She hit ignore. She had to do this; she had to put herself first so she wouldn't be crushed in the end. "I love you Benny," she whispered to the empty room, "but this time, I have to love myself more."

CHAPTER TWENTY-THREE

Sophie woke with a start as if she'd been shaken from a nightmare, but she couldn't remember having any dreams. Her mouth felt dry and her head felt fuzzy. Had she drunk herself to sleep the night before? She didn't think so, but she couldn't remember.

She scrubbed her face with the palm of her hand, willing herself to fully wake up. When she lowered her hand, she sighed and finally took a good look at her room. Her brows creased in confusion. She wasn't in her room. Her first thought was that she was still asleep then she guessed maybe she had too much to drink the night before and somehow ended up where she didn't belong, and then panic finally set in. The room was sparse, a simple dresser in one corner, and the bed she was lying on. She was still fully dressed in the clothes she had on the night before.

She took deep breaths to calm her racing heart. Wherever she was, she'd figure a way out, but she needed not to panic in order to do so. She had just finished having a mental pep talk with herself when the door to her room opened. She moved back farther on the bed instinctively, the need to protect herself overpowering the false confidence she had just built.

And then she gasped. "Benny?"

"Hey Soph, I thought I heard movement in here, so I figured I'd check on you."

"Where am I?" she asked, still nervous, but no longer alarmed. "And how did I get here?"

"Come with me and I'll show you around. You can get cleaned up in the bathroom and then we can talk."

"What the hell are you talking about? Where are we?" She still wasn't afraid, but she was starting to get upset.

"I guess that depends on how things go. This might be a temporary situation or this could be your new home."

"My what?" she asked incredulously. "Benjamin Ian Negrete, start talking," she demanded.

"Still difficult," he mumbled. "Okay, this used to be Kat's room."

"Kat's room?" she asked. "But this isn't their home," she protested.

"Yeah, Mason and Kat decided to keep this place because it was where it all started. Sentimental stuff. Came in pretty handy for me, though."

"This is…" she trailed off as realization dawned on her. She jumped out of bed and raced toward Benny, her fists pounding on his chest. "You kidnapped me!" she screamed.

He grabbed her hands in his and looked into her eyes. "You were avoiding me and pulling away from me."

"You can't keep me here," she told him, her breaths shallow as she tried to wiggle free from his grasp.

"Actually," he smirked, "I can. All the windows are locked, the doors only open if you're authorized to open them, and well…you're not. The place is soundproof. There's nothing dangerous in here that you can use to hurt me and get me to open it up, not that I think you'd do that, but just letting you know."

"How long do you think that you can keep me here?" she asked as she stopped struggling in his hold, understanding that she truly wasn't going anywhere if he didn't want her to.

"Forever if I have to," he responded, and the tone of his voice made her realize he was serious. "But I only want to get to the bottom of what's going on with us. One minute we're happy, and the next, you're pushing me away." She heard the sorrow in his voice and she actually felt a tiny bit of guilt. "I needed to be able to talk to you, to get you to deal with whatever is going on. And this," he waved his hand around the room, "was the best thing I could think of."

"You can't do this," she whispered but knew her words were false.

"I already did, Soph. The sooner you tell me what's wrong, the sooner we can deal with it, and then we'll both be out of here."

"I can't," she answered softly. "I'm sorry, Benny, but I can't."

"Then I guess we're both in here for the long haul," he told her as he released her hands and walked out.

Sophie stumbled back until she fell on the bed; she closed her eyes and let the tears trail down her cheeks. She had secretly wanted Benny to find a way to break through her barriers, and this was certainly doing just that, but at the same time, she couldn't let him break *her*. She was afraid that if she gave in and told him that she loved him then she wouldn't be able to leave before he broke her heart, and she knew he'd break it. Not necessarily because he was a bad guy or because he didn't care about her, but simply because the people she loved always left. It was her burden alone. She spent the next half hour sitting in that same position before she found the courage to get up.

She found some of her clothes in the drawers and when she wandered into the hallway, it took only one try before she found the bathroom. When she made it to the kitchen, Benny was making breakfast.

"Waffles with strawberries, your favorite," he told her as he set it down in front of her.

"Thank you," she murmured as her heart cracked just a little more. If he kept doing things like that, even as he held her hostage – which was insane, *insane* – she was going to fall even harder for him.

They ate in tense silence. Sophie started to get up to do the dishes when Benny slammed his fork down on the plate. "No," he yelled. "We're not going to pretend like we're a happy little family. The good little wifey does the dishes after breakfast," he mocked. "I kidnapped you, Sophie," he roared. "I kidnapped you." He repeated it, but his words were full of both shock and defeat. "We're going to fix this. We're going to fix this right now." He stood up abruptly then as if trying to figure out what to do or what to say. Then he walked over to her before pulling her to the couch so they could sit facing each other, almost touching, but not quite.

"This is big, Soph. This is pretty fucking big," he waved his hand around the room. "I just kidnapped you," he emphasized again. "Doesn't that say something to you? I'm willing to go to great lengths just so we can figure this out. I need to figure this out. I need *you*."
Sophie's heart was breaking, cracking wide open, and she wasn't sure if she was the one responsible for that or if it was Benny's doing. She started shivering, not because she was cold but because his words were getting to her, his words were penetrating her very core. She opened her mouth to say something, say anything, but nothing came out.

"Dammit, Sophie! Talk to me." He rarely used her full name lately, and the fact that he just did it twice in the last five minutes really meant something.

She found her voice, but the words she spoke were out of fear for her own heart. "I can't, Benny. I just can't. And I can't be with you. We need to end things, and you need to let me out."

"I can't do that," Benny responded.

"Please Benny, please let me go."

Benny let out a humorous laugh. "You know," he paused, "Kat asked Mason to let her go, and one day, he did. Look how that turned out."

"I'm not Kat. You can't keep me here!" she yelled. "I don't want to be here. I don't want to be with you," she told him as her voice cracked.

"You're lying, Sophie. I know you are. Something happened, something that's affecting you. I want to help you. I want to help us."

"You can't!" she screamed.

"Goddamn, Soph!" he shouted. "I fucking love you, and you're breaking in front of me, and I can't do anything about it because you won't let me."

Sophie's heart beat frantically. He didn't mean it; he couldn't mean it. "You what?" she asked.

"Shit, sorry, it wasn't meant to come out like that. It's just that...I don't know what to do. I don't know how to fix whatever is broken if you won't help me."

"Don't say that," she croaked. "Don't say that. You don't love me."

Benny stood and moved to kneel in front of her. "Look into my eyes, Sophie. I love you so much. I love you so fucking much. All this...it's because I can't let you go. I don't expect you to love me. And if you tell me right now that you don't care about me, that you really and truly don't want to be with me, I will open that door, watch you walk out, and you'll never have to hear from me again. Tell me that it's what you want and I'll do it. It will kill me, but I'll do it."

He lifted a finger to wipe the tears that were pouring onto her cheeks. She hadn't bothered to brush them away because there were just too many. She was fighting not to sob in front of him, but she couldn't stop from crying.

She stood up and moved away from him, causing him to stand and face her. They stood an arm's length away as if preparing for battle. Maybe that was exactly what they were doing.

"Don't you see, Benny? That's the problem."

"I don't understand what you mean," Benny told her.

"I don't want you to leave me, but you will. Everyone I love does. Ethan...my baby...even my parents moved away. I can't lose you, too. I won't!"

"You'll never lose me," he told her.

"I will!" she yelled and moved back as he stepped toward her.

"Soph, baby, I'm not going anywhere."

"Everyone I love goes! Everyone leaves me!"

"Not me. I'll never leave you," he told her.

"It's not in your control," she cried harder now.

"Sophie, you love me?" he asked.

"That's why I have to go before you break my heart!" she responded.

"Tell me, Soph. Tell me you love me."

"I love you, Benny," she wailed, the words hurting her almost as much as her shattering heart. "And now I want you to let me go. You *need* to let me go."

He tried to grab her, but she moved further back and put her hand up to stop him.

"Why are you doing this?" Benny asked. "You love me, I love you. I don't want to leave you, and you clearly don't want to leave me. What are you afraid of?"

"I can't survive losing you, too!"

"You won't, Sophie. You have me forever," he told her as he pulled his shirt over his head. She covered her mouth with her hand as she focused on his chest. Right above the missing puzzle piece tattoo was a new one.

"You see this, Soph, this is you," he told her as he pointed to the tattoo. It was the missing puzzle piece. It fit Ethan's piece perfectly, but this time, it was made to look like it was set on top of his skin, the shading so perfect that it looked like a real puzzle piece. And written across the piece was her name in beautiful script.

"When Ethan died, a part of me died with him. This tattoo," he pointed to the missing piece, "was the part of my heart that he took with him to the grave. Ever since, I've been living with a hole in my heart. But I've found the missing piece, Sophie. I've found it with you. You fill my heart and make it whole. Only you can do that. My heart belongs to you and only you for eternity."

"Benny," she whispered, her sobs coming stronger now. She could just see a light pink tinge around the tattoo through the haze of tears. He had gotten it recently. He had marked his skin permanently with her even when he knew he was losing her. He was hers. He was well and truly hers, and he wasn't going anywhere.

"I wasn't going to do this like this," he whispered. "But I guess now's as good a time as any," he said more to himself than to her. "I can't promise you that I will live forever, Soph, and I know that scares you, but I can promise you that for as long as I live and then some, I will love you like no other. And if our days end up being numbered, I will make sure you don't regret them, and that they are worth it. I'll give you so many happy memories that you'll never feel alone even if I'm not there. I'll do everything I can to make you smile on a daily basis. No, scratch that, on an hourly basis, every single minute. And if you cry, I sure as hell hope they'll be happy tears. I'm yours, Sophie, and I sure as hell hope you will be mine," he said as he pulled a small black box from his pocket.

He told her the only words that could put a fracture in her stone wall. "I need you to let go of the past." She felt the crack start to spread. "I need you to let it go so we can build a future together." The first bricks started to fall as she took in his words. "Will you let it go, Sophie, so you can let me in?" And the wall fell. He opened the box, and an oval diamond sparkled, surrounded by smaller diamonds in a rose gold setting, catching the light and looking like the sun setting on the horizon. "Will you let me show you that I'm not going anywhere? Will you be mine, Sophie Basi? Please say you'll marry me."

She was frozen, paralyzed in place. Her fear had disappeared almost as quickly as it came. Benny was right. She couldn't control life and death, but being with him – for any amount of time – would be worth it. She looked into Benny's nervous face, the insecurities written across his face as clearly as her own. And then she knew, she just knew…she'd happily risk losing this man as long as she could even have just one more day with him.

"Yes," she screamed as she fell into his arms. They fell backward, but Benny cushioned their fall, just like she knew he'd always do.

"Yes?" he asked.

"I love you, Benny, and I'd love to be your wife."

"I love you so much," he growled as he captured her lips, his mouth searing hers. "I love you, Sophie Basi, and I'm not letting you go."

"Never."

EPILOGUE

"I can't believe he's all grown up," Kat sniffled next to Sophie.

"Kitty Kat, sorry to tell you, but Eddie's been grown for quite some time," Benny told her.

"But he was just this little lanky kid when I met him, and now," Kat pointed toward Eddie, "look at him."

Eddie was off to the side, appeasing his mom by letting her take pictures of him, but his eyes kept roaming over the girl who was to his right. Sophie had learned about Eddie's past from Kat and Benny, and even met Samantha, Eddie's mom, on numerous occasions. She'd have never known that she was a reformed addict if Benny hadn't assured her. She didn't drink, worked as a receptionist, and seemed to be doing well.

"Yeah, I'm not so sure about that whole grown-up thing," Sophie laughed just as she saw Eddie wink at the girl.

It was Eddie's graduation day from Princeton, and everyone was in high spirits. They had screamed their hearts out when Eddie was called up. Even quiet John, who was now chatting it up with some female professor. It had even topped the day they found out Eddie had gotten into the USC Keck School of Medicine. "Now will you tutor me?" Eddie had asked Sophie.

"I'm so happy for you. I'm tempted to say yes," she told him.

"Don't do it, Soph," Benny told her. "Stay strong." They all got a good laugh.

"You hush," Kat mock scolded Sophie, bringing her back the present.

"Kat, he's not the shy guy he was back then," Mason reminded her.

"But I don't want him to grow up!" Kat whined.

"That's what you said about Benji and Katy last week," Sophie snorted. "And they're three!"

Kat opened her mouth to obviously protest, but Mason spoke before she had a chance to. "Come on, Kat, let's go get some pictures, too." She beamed and he dragged her away.

Sophie turned to her husband and smiled. They had been married for just over a year, but it still made her heart flutter when she thought of him as her husband.

After she had said yes, they ended up staying in the infamous *Kidnap Club*, as Sophie referred to it, for three more days. They talked through the past, through her fears, even his insecurities, and of course, they barely left the bed. After that, though, they had to go back to their normal lives, but Benny refused to let any more time slip away from them. He convinced her to marry him almost immediately. If Benny'd had his way, they would have flown to Vegas that weekend, but she told him that although she wanted a small wedding, she still wanted a real wedding. He gave her one month. Thank God for Kat because she wouldn't have been able to pull off a wedding in one month, but when Kat heard, after she let out an ear-piercing scream, she became a wedding planner drill sergeant.

"I know the perfect place!" she told her, and she had been right. They were married in a small restaurant that was high on a cliff with glass windows that overlooked the entire city. They had only about thirty people there, but it was exactly what she wanted. It was intimate and perfect. Her parents had assumed that she was pregnant, but she assured them she just had firsthand knowledge that time was short and not to waste any of it. It took them a few days to come around to the idea that their girl was marrying "troublemaker" Benny, but he called and had a lengthy conversation with them. He shooed Sophie away when she tried to listen in, but she heard little snippets about how much he loved her, how he'd never do anything to hurt her, and he knew he wasn't worthy of her love, but he'd spend the rest of his life trying to be. Her heart broke when she heard that, and it took a lot of self-restraint not to barge into the room and tell him that he *was* worthy.

Needless to say, they told Sophie that they approved. She wore an ivory satin gown that flowed near the bottom like a classy ballgown. Light crystals adorned the torso and the sweetheart neckline as well as the very bottom. She wore her hair up with a fishnet veil that covered only the side of her face. She had gone for old Hollywood glam, and from the look on Benny's face when he saw her, it had worked.

"Holy shit, Soph. How am I going to survive until we're alone?" he had asked her. "You look un-fucking-believable." *He was so sweet when he needed to be.*

They lived at his place for about another month while they looked for a place to move into together, and then Benny came home and told her he had a surprise. He drove her two blocks away from Kat and Mason's home and before she even saw the place, she knew it was the one. It had been perfect inside, too, not to mention the fact that she loved she'd always be near Kat.

There were times she became nervous that Benny would leave her, and there were times that she'd see the shadows pass his eyes and knew he was thinking about Ethan, but they were strong together.

"He's a good kid, huh?" Benny asked her motioning toward Eddie.

"Yeah, he is," Sophie agreed.

"But he'd better stop hitting on my wife or I'm going to have to hand him his ass."

"Now that's not a very fatherly thing to do." She smiled.

"Nah, Mason's more like his dad than me," Benny responded. "Not saying I wouldn't make a fucking great father," Benny smirked. "Have you seen me with Benji and Katy?" he bragged.

"You'll make an amazing father," Sophie agreed. "But maybe you should start laying off the cussing…at least in the next eight months," she added as she laid a hand on her stomach.

"Eight months," he repeated as her words dawned on him. "You're? I'm? We're?" He couldn't finish a sentence and Sophie smiled wider.

"We're pregnant," she whispered.

The words were barely out of her mouth before Benny swooped her in his arms and kissed her fiercely. "We're gonna have a baby!" he cried out as they broke apart. "We're having a baby!" he screamed again. Suddenly, they were surrounded by their friends, who were hugging them and wishing them well.

"And I thought today couldn't get any better," Kat told them.

Benny wrapped his arms around Sophie. "Thank you, Soph. Thank you for letting me into your life, for marrying me, for giving me this gift. Thank you for letting me love you."

"I love you, Benny," she whispered as she laid a kiss on his lips. "You know," she told him, "this all started because you didn't let go."

"And I never will."

~The End~

Liked Benny's Story?
See where it all began. Read on for a preview of Kat and
Mason's story.

Let Me Go
By DC Renee

PROLOGUE

His accuser. All he had to keep him company for the last six years was her name and a vague image in his mind; those details had been seared into his mind for him to mull over. He never got to see the realization dawn on her face when she comprehended that she had picked out the wrong guy. He wasn't even sure if what she accused him of had truly happened to her. Whether she had gotten the wrong guy or had just focused on him and lied. He had a feeling it was the latter. And it was that gut feeling that burrowed its way into the depths of his soul and stewed there, waiting to erupt, waiting for the chance to explode.

And now that chance was about to present itself. He had planned it all perfectly. Finalized the details with precision, thinking of every little thing that could go wrong. But, then again, that was what he had done in his former life. He had been a doctor, one of the best. He graduated from Harvard at the top of his class, became one of the youngest doctors to lead a department, and went on to lead several departments. He was skilled; it was like second nature to him. The body was like a puzzle, waiting to be put back together, and he was a master at puzzles.

He was good looking, six feet tall with shockingly black hair that he always kept short but messy, deep green eyes, straight nose, strong jawline, and even perfect teeth, thanks to braces in junior high. He knew he was a looker and always used that to his advantage.

He had never had time for relationships, but he definitely loved the company of women. Lots of women. He never took advantage of a woman; his looks got him whatever he wanted or needed. He justified his actions because he was always up-front about the fact that he wasn't looking for more than just sex. It didn't stop some women from calling him every name in the book. So his womanizing reputation preceded him, but he didn't care. He had a fantastic home in an upscale neighborhood and the respect of all his peers and friends. His parents, unfortunately, had died in a car accident while he was still in college, but he knew they were smiling down on him with pride. They had been wealthy, coming from "old money" that he had inherited, but his career also helped increase his worth. He was on top of the world until, one night after a thirty-six hour shift, he was awoken from his much needed sleep after only hours of snoozing by loud knocking on his door.

Rape. One damn word changed his life.

He was accused of rape. He lived alone, had no good alibi, and somehow his hair was found on the victim. How it got there, he could only guess. She had positively identified him from one of those line-ups like they show on the television. The prosecution had a flimsy case, but it seemed like the jury was hell-bent on convicting the good-looking, hard-working doctor. His memory of what she looked like was fuzzy at best, but that was probably his own imagination as the entire trial was a blur. His mind was reeling the entire time at the realization of his situation. He had the finest lawyers defending him and his sanity, spending an absurd amount of money. But in the end it wasn't enough, he was still convicted of rape. Something he couldn't ever fathom coming close to doing. He had seen the ugliness of such a crime numerous times in the hospital, and it left a person with not just physical scars but mental ones as well. The trial and subsequent prison time had left him with mental and physical scars of his own.

He was sentenced to twelve years, and all appeals were denied. He only served five years, getting out a year ago on good behavior. When he went to prison, he was a normal, sane person, never capable of truly hurting someone. But spending five years in prison, while being labeled a rapist, was enough to make anyone crack. The scars he now wore were the same as those he had seen in the hospital, both physical and mental. Inmates aren't too keen on rapists, especially pretty-boy ones. And he learned that the hard way.

During that time in prison, he held onto the name of his accuser and that blurry image of her, his hatred increasing with each passing day and each brutal violation to his own body. She did this to him. And now she was going to know what it was like to have her life stripped from her and humiliated every day. Now, a year after his release, he was ready to make his move. Mason Tredwell was ready to find Kat Gingham.

Want more books by DC Renee?

Read on for a preview of A Brutal Betrayal

Out October 2014

PROLOGUE

"No, God, please. No!" she screamed, her voice hoarse from the screaming and begging, her face tear stained and bruised. No one could hear her in the dark alley, no one cared. Her pleas were drowned out by the sounds of the traffic nearby and the music vibrating through the many clubs in the area.

She felt like she had been crying out for hours, but it had probably been no more than a few minutes. Her assailant had her hair in a tight grip, the roots on the verge of being torn out. The rough surface of the wall cut into her cheek as she was pressed against it. The biting pain was nothing compared to the terrifying violation being forced upon her.

With his face buried in her neck, she could feel his hot breath coming out in small puffs with each thrust. He was mumbling, but she couldn't hear his words over the thunderous roar of blood in her head or the sound of skin slapping on skin.

"Please, stop, please," she whimpered, her voice almost gone at this point. She closed her eyes, willing the pain to stop, willing the violation to end, willing her mind to leave her body behind.

Three hours ago, she had told her parents she was spending the night with a friend, which wasn't a total lie. She just hadn't told them that she and her friend would be utilizing their new fake IDs to go to some clubs first. Her friend's parents were out of town, so no one would notice or disturb them. They took advantage and drank at the house first before taking a cab to the main street where all the bars and clubs were located. Making their way through three clubs quickly, they picked up free drinks from men who assumed they were much older than they were. Twenty minutes before, things changed when she lost her friend in the crowd. The booming music and the throngs of people, bodies pressed against each other, writhing to the notes coming from the loud speakers, immersing themselves in the beauty of letting go. With the added relaxation from the drinks she'd had, she let go, maybe too much, only to realize that she was without her friend, groping and being groped without the safety of someone she knew. She needed air. *Just a little*, she told herself. She would step out for just a moment, maybe text or call her friend. Worst case, she could always grab a cab back to her friend's place and wait it out.

She had stood by the door of the last club, sucking in clean air. Well, cleaner than the musty air from inside. Her head was still throbbing from the pounding music. She didn't hear him approach. She hadn't realized what was going on until she was pressed against the wall, until the hands pushing her face into the wall felt wrong, violent.

"Don't make a sound," he had said, his voice low and gravely, and the enormity of the situation hit her. She didn't listen, she screamed, a loud, shrieking sound coming from her lips. He punched her, slamming her head against the corrosive wall. She didn't care, that was better than what she knew would happen. She screamed again, and he pushed her into the wall, hard. She bucked into him, trying to push him away. Her arms flailed where he hadn't pinned them down, trying to scratch him somehow, although she knew she couldn't reach him at this angle. He got a hold of her arms and pinned them in front of her and pushed her against the wall. She felt her lip starting to swell, and her body felt like someone had snapped it in two. But still, that kind of pain would heal. The pain she knew he intended on inflicting would not, so she didn't care. She didn't stop screaming. Not when he lifted her dress, not when he tore her underwear like it was a piece of tissue paper, not when his rough, calloused hands pinned her hips to the wall, not when he forced himself inside her, not when he pounded away the remnants of her innocence, not when he continued to violate every part of her being.

"Please stop. No. Please, don't do this." Her lips moved, even as her voice disappeared. But it didn't matter. He was doing it. He had done it. She felt the pain, the ache in every crevice and corner of her body, in every niche of her mind. And he had been rough. He had beaten her to get this. She could feel the telltale signs of bruising all along her body. But she could have taken that. He continued to mumble, the words still incoherent to her, but she finally felt herself starting to check out from this time and space. Her mind was finally starting to protect her, pulling her out of the moment. The numbness began to take over, but just before she lost consciousness of the here and now, she felt his body tense, and he went rigid with his release. She vaguely felt him push her down to the floor when he was done with her. She barely remembered hearing the zipper on what she assumed were his jeans. And she only just understood that the sounds of footsteps were his as he ran away from her, leaving her there bloody and broken, used and discarded, sullied and ashamed.

COMING SOON:

Three Loving Words

I hate you. I heard those words so many times from his mouth that they lost their meaning. His "three loving words" is how I mockingly referred to them. It didn't bother me, though, because I hated him, too.

He was gorgeous, with dark tousled hair, full lips, a strong jaw, and a body deserving of a magazine cover. He was rich and cared for his mother deeply. On paper, he was the perfect husband. The problem? He was *my* husband.

I dreamed of a fairytale love story for as long as I could remember. I dreamed of a boy to fall head over heels for me and treat me like the sun rose and set at my feet, especially after living in the shadow of my perfect sister and never feeling good enough for my family. When I decided to earn my parents' love in a dramatic fashion, I'll admit that I never imagined marrying him would end up part of the bargain.

The kicker? Enzo Faust didn't want to marry me, either. And yet, here we are, a man that I both fear and loathe is my "I do...for better or worse." I just didn't anticipate that it'd be more 'worse' than 'better.'

I'm Paige Stiles, and here's my story.

Made in the USA
Las Vegas, NV
12 February 2022

43806742R00069